MARVEL

SPIDER-HAM

GREAT POWER, NO RESPONSIBILITY

AN ORIGINAL GRAPHIC NOVEL

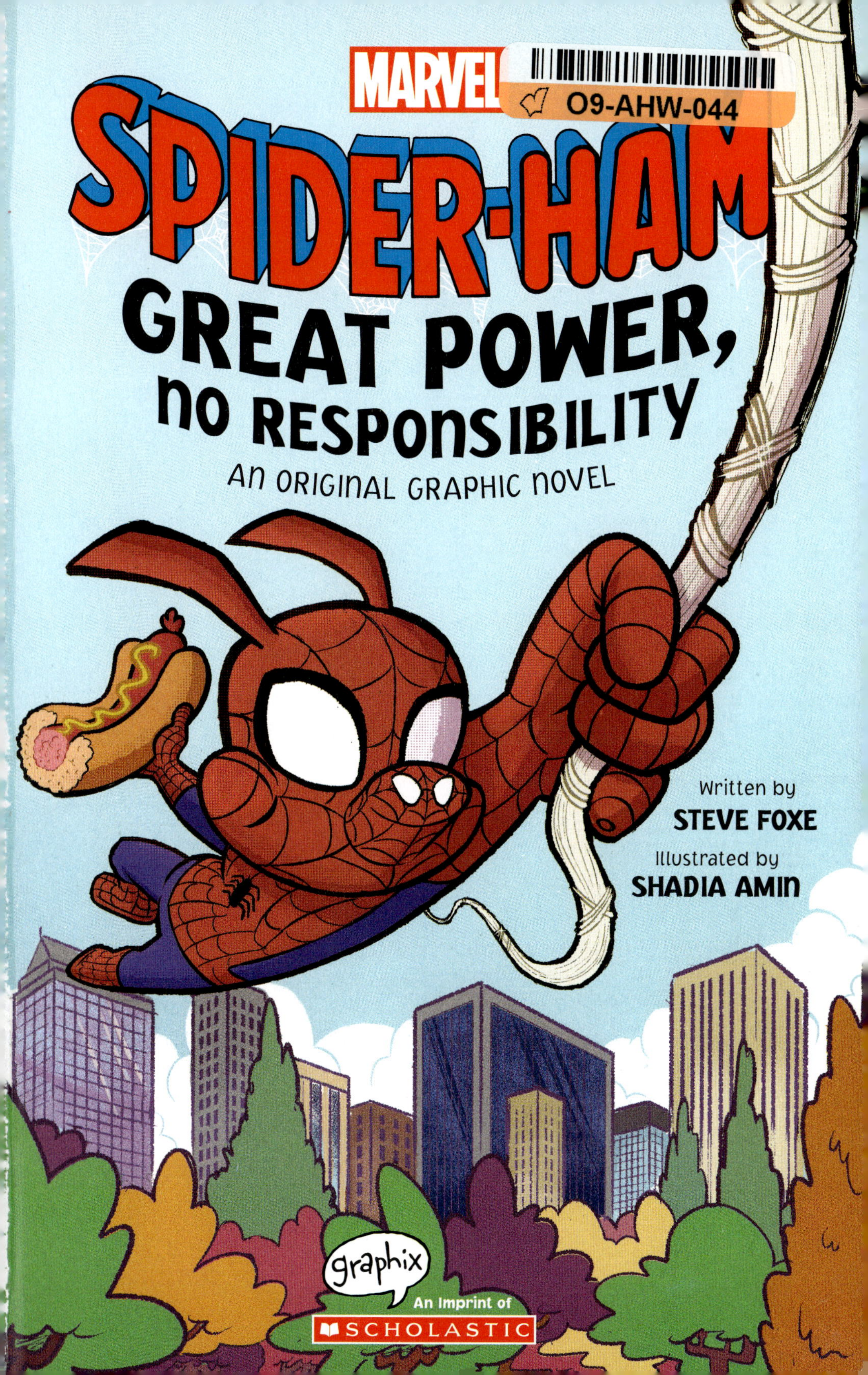

Written by
STEVE FOXE
Illustrated by
SHADIA AMIN

graphix
An Imprint of
SCHOLASTIC

All rights reserved. Published by Graphix, an imprint of Scholastic Inc., *Publishers since 1920*. SCHOLASTIC, GRAPHIX, and associated logos are trademarks and/or registered trademarks of Scholastic Inc.

ISBN 978-1-338-73431-7 (hardcover)
ISBN 978-1-338-73430-0 (paperback)

10 9 8 7 6 5 4 3 2 1   21 22 23 24 25
Printed in China   62

First edition, October 2021

Artwork by Shadia Amin
Edited by Michael Petranek
Lettering by Rae Crawford
Book design by Jess Meltzer

Lauren Bisom, Editor, Juvenile Publishing
Caitlin O'Connell, Associate Editor
Sven Larsen, VP Licensed Publishing
C.B. Cebulski, Editor in Chief

CHAPTER ONE:

SOW-WY 'BOUT IT

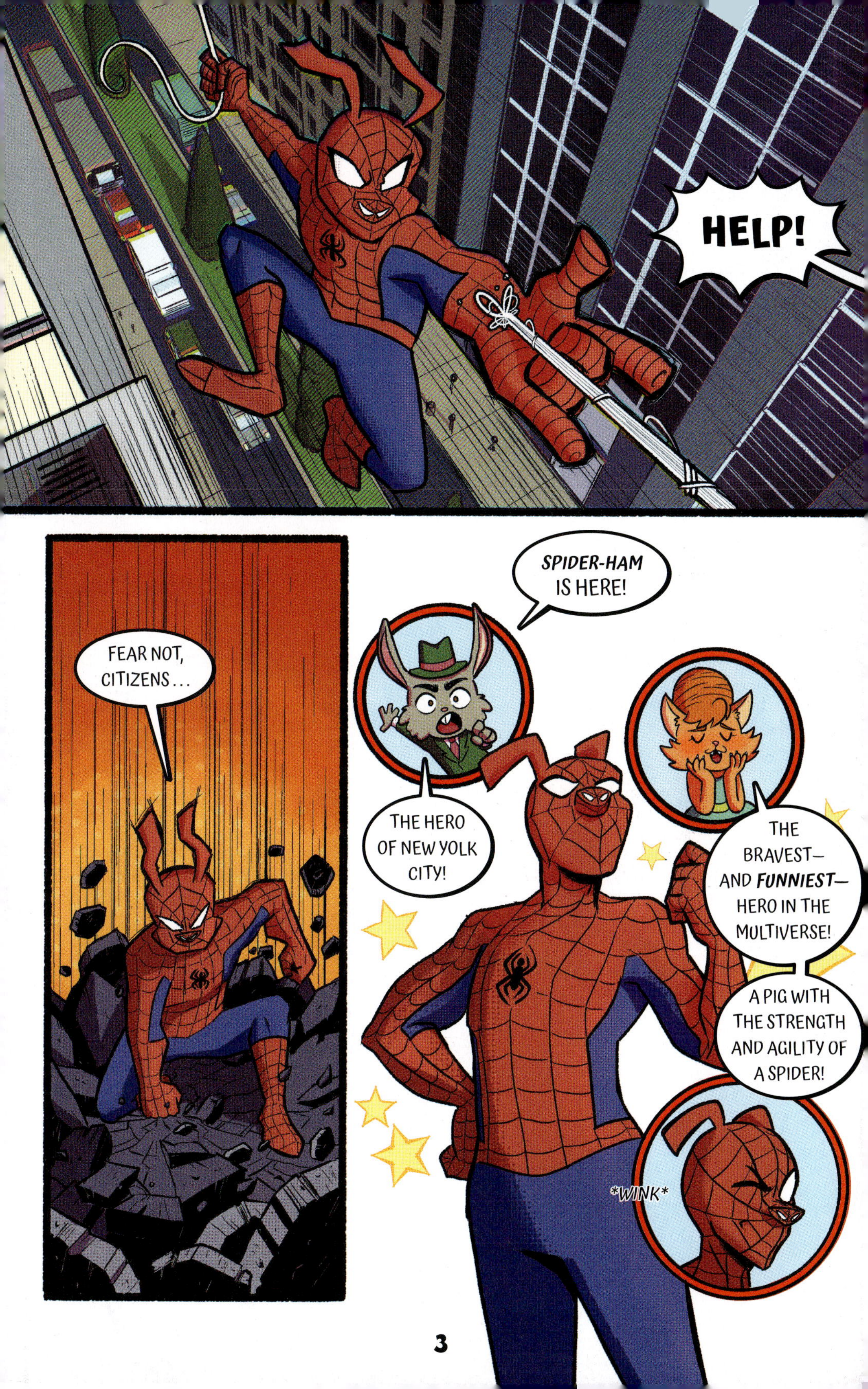
HELP!
FEAR NOT, CITIZENS . . .
SPIDER-HAM IS HERE!
THE HERO OF NEW YOLK CITY!
THE BRAVEST— AND FUNNIEST— HERO IN THE MULTIVERSE!
A PIG WITH THE STRENGTH AND AGILITY OF A SPIDER!
WINK

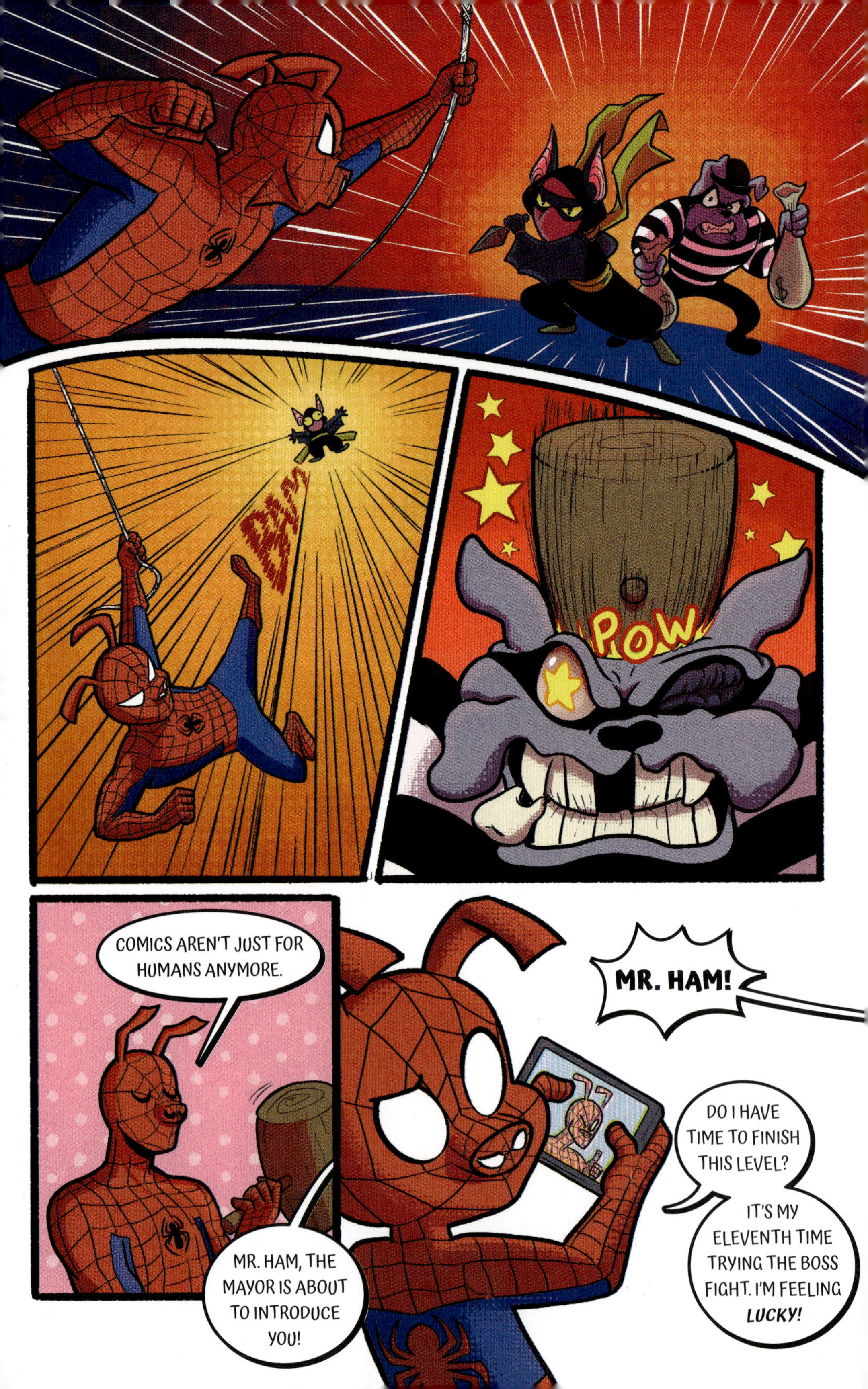
POW
COMICS AREN'T JUST FOR HUMANS ANYMORE.
MR. HAM!
MR. HAM, THE MAYOR IS ABOUT TO INTRODUCE YOU!
DO I HAVE TIME TO FINISH THIS LEVEL?
IT'S MY ELEVENTH TIME TRYING THE BOSS FIGHT. I'M FEELING ***LUCKY!***

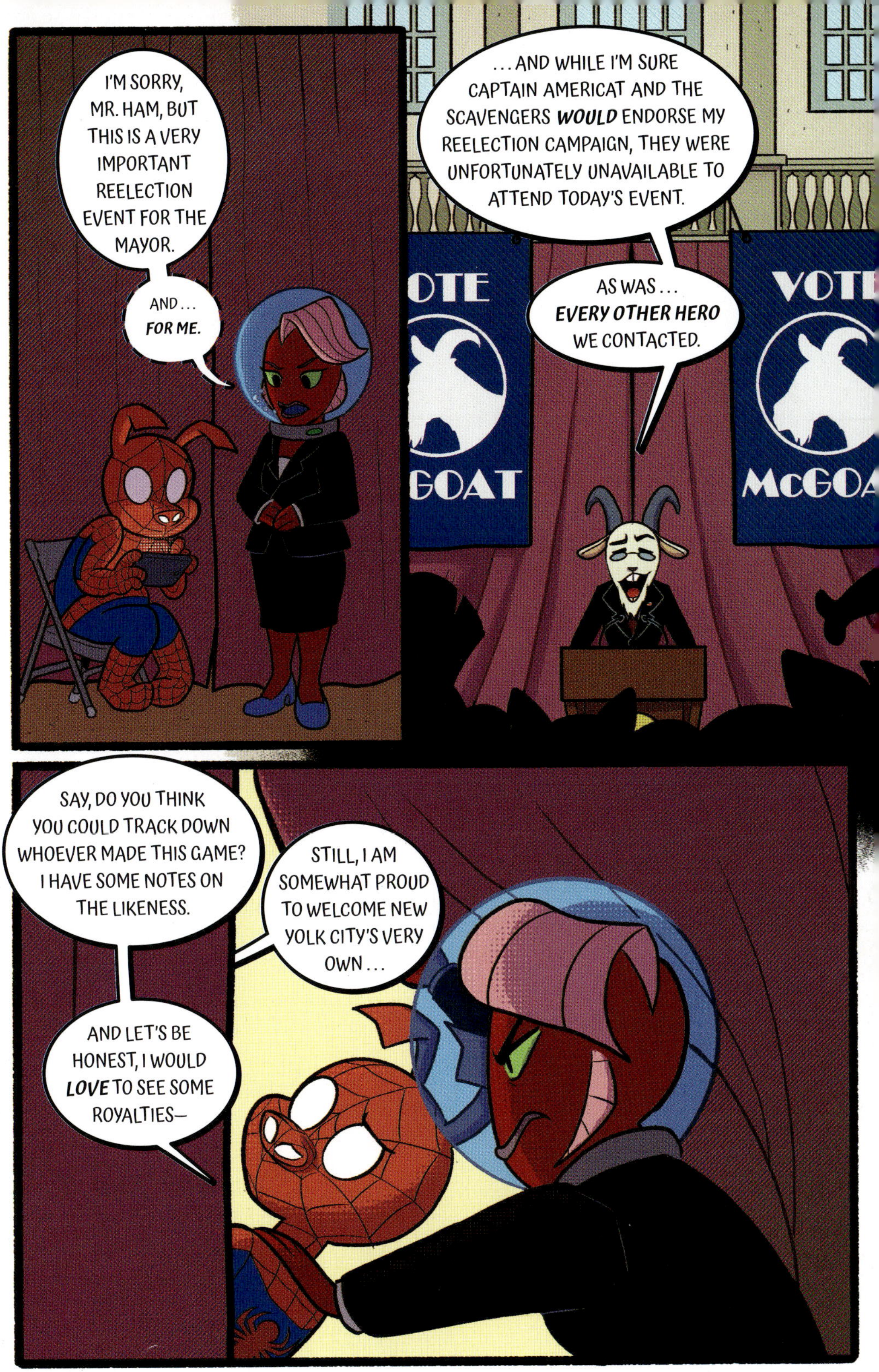
I'M SORRY, MR. HAM, BUT THIS IS A VERY IMPORTANT REELECTION EVENT FOR THE MAYOR.
AND... FOR ME.
...AND WHILE I'M SURE CAPTAIN AMERICAT AND THE SCAVENGERS WOULD ENDORSE MY REELECTION CAMPAIGN, THEY WERE UNFORTUNATELY UNAVAILABLE TO ATTEND TODAY'S EVENT.
AS WAS... EVERY OTHER HERO WE CONTACTED.
SAY, DO YOU THINK YOU COULD TRACK DOWN WHOEVER MADE THIS GAME? I HAVE SOME NOTES ON THE LIKENESS.
STILL, I AM SOMEWHAT PROUD TO WELCOME NEW YOLK CITY'S VERY OWN...
AND LET'S BE HONEST, I WOULD LOVE TO SEE SOME ROYALTIES—

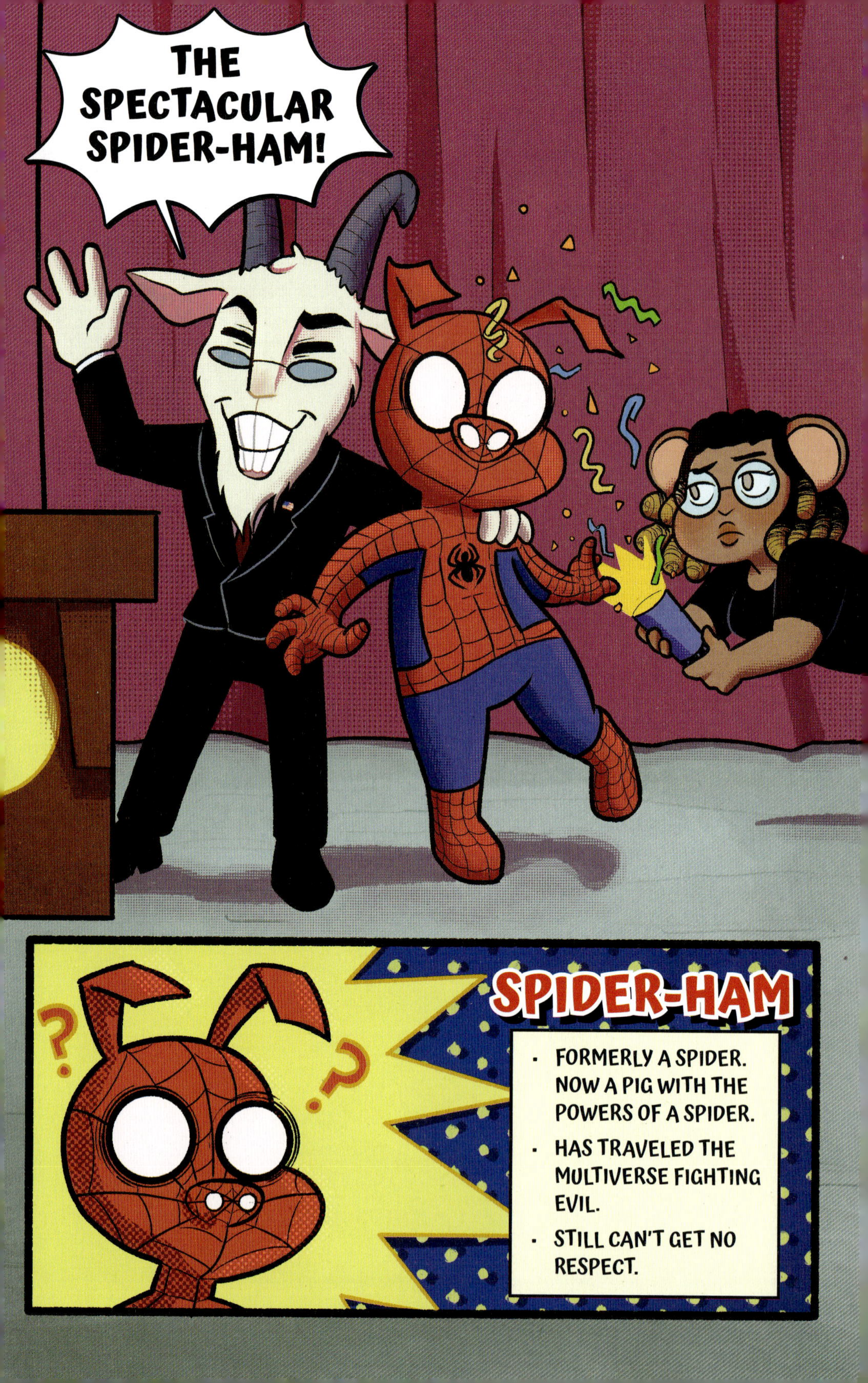
THE SPECTACULAR SPIDER-HAM!
?
?
SPIDER-HAM
FORMERLY A SPIDER. NOW A PIG WITH THE POWERS OF A SPIDER.
HAS TRAVELED THE MULTIVERSE FIGHTING EVIL.
STILL CAN'T GET NO RESPECT.

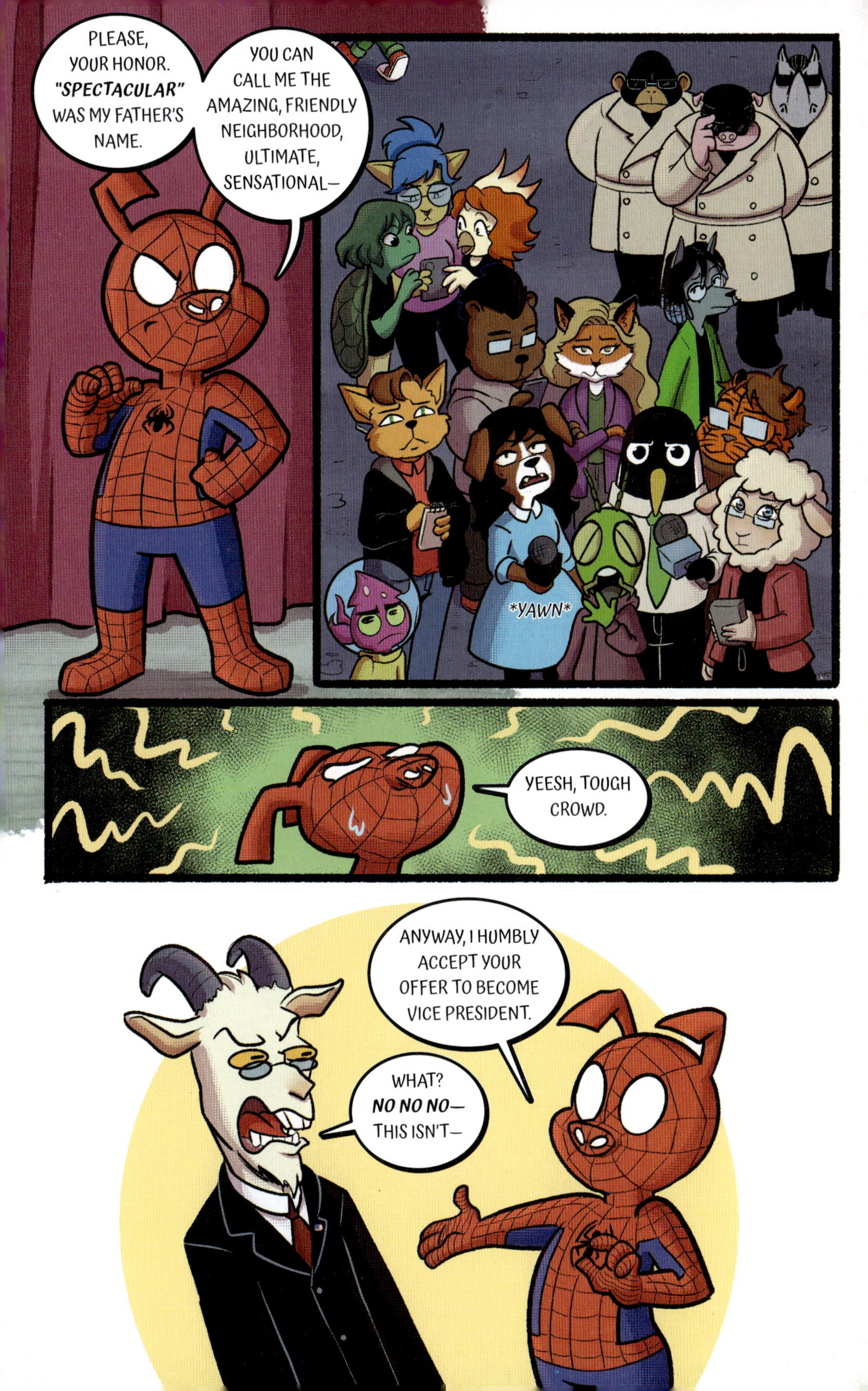
PLEASE, YOUR HONOR. **"SPECTACULAR"** WAS MY FATHER'S NAME.
YOU CAN CALL ME THE AMAZING, FRIENDLY NEIGHBORHOOD, ULTIMATE, SENSATIONAL—
YAWN
YEESH, TOUGH CROWD.
ANYWAY, I HUMBLY ACCEPT YOUR OFFER TO BECOME VICE PRESIDENT.
WHAT? ***NO NO NO***— THIS ISN'T—

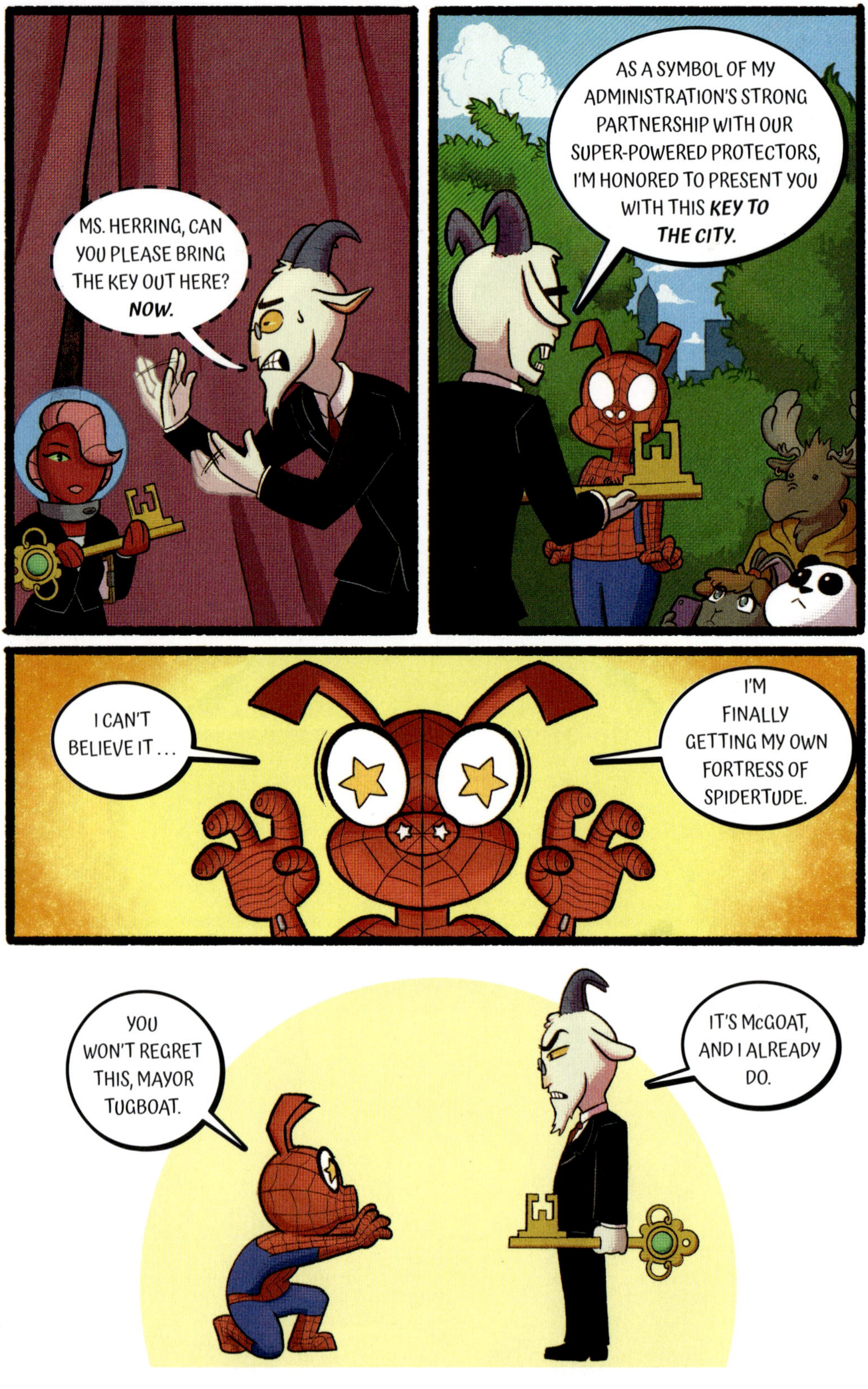
MS. HERRING, CAN YOU PLEASE BRING THE KEY OUT HERE? **NOW.**
AS A SYMBOL OF MY ADMINISTRATION'S STRONG PARTNERSHIP WITH OUR SUPER-POWERED PROTECTORS, I'M HONORED TO PRESENT YOU WITH THIS **KEY TO THE CITY.**
I CAN'T BELIEVE IT . . .
I'M FINALLY GETTING MY OWN FORTRESS OF SPIDERTUDE.
YOU WON'T REGRET THIS, MAYOR TUGBOAT.
IT'S McGOAT, AND I ALREADY DO.

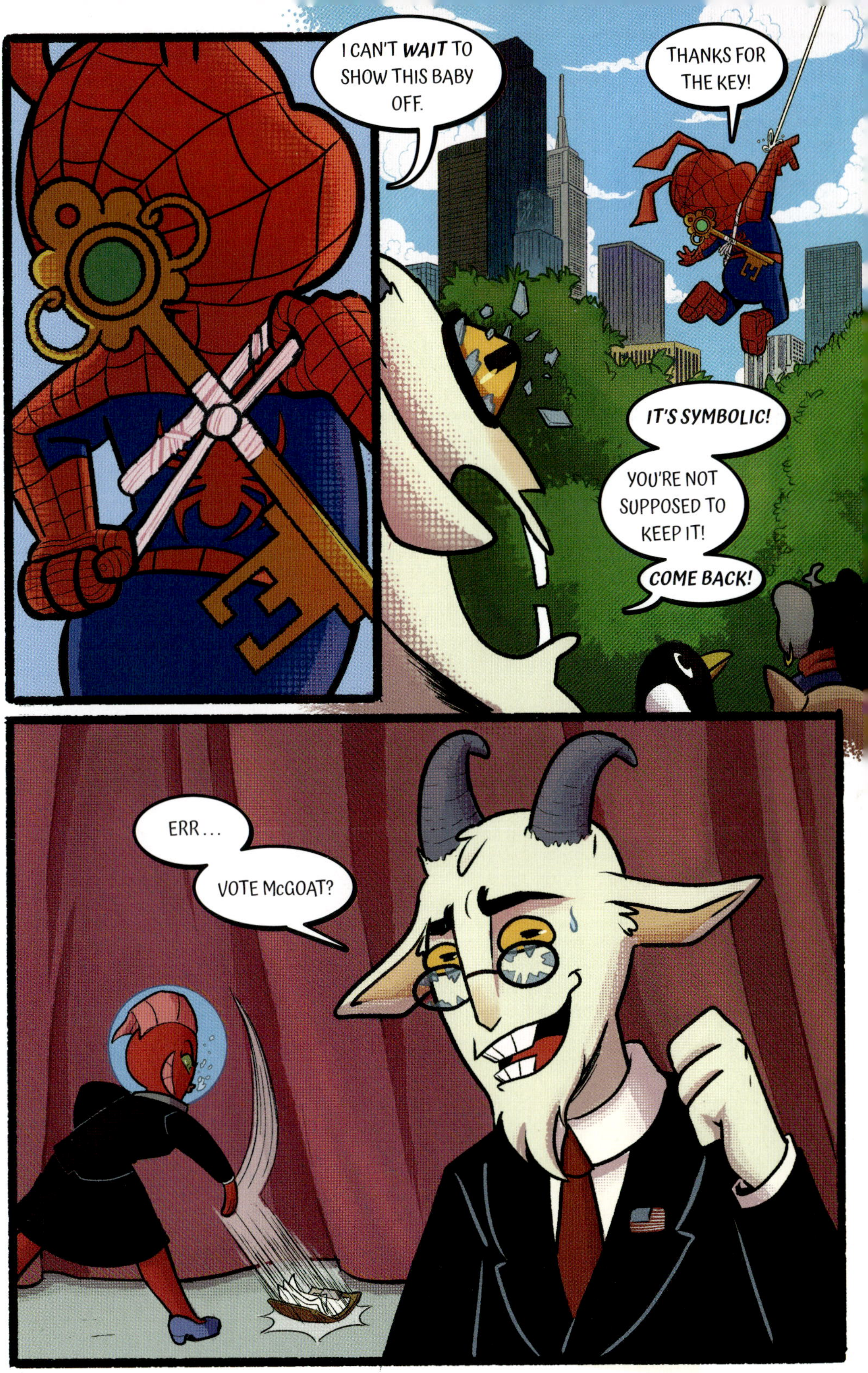
I CAN'T **WAIT** TO SHOW THIS BABY OFF.
THANKS FOR THE KEY!
IT'S SYMBOLIC!
YOU'RE NOT SUPPOSED TO KEEP IT!
COME BACK!
ERR . . .
VOTE McGOAT?

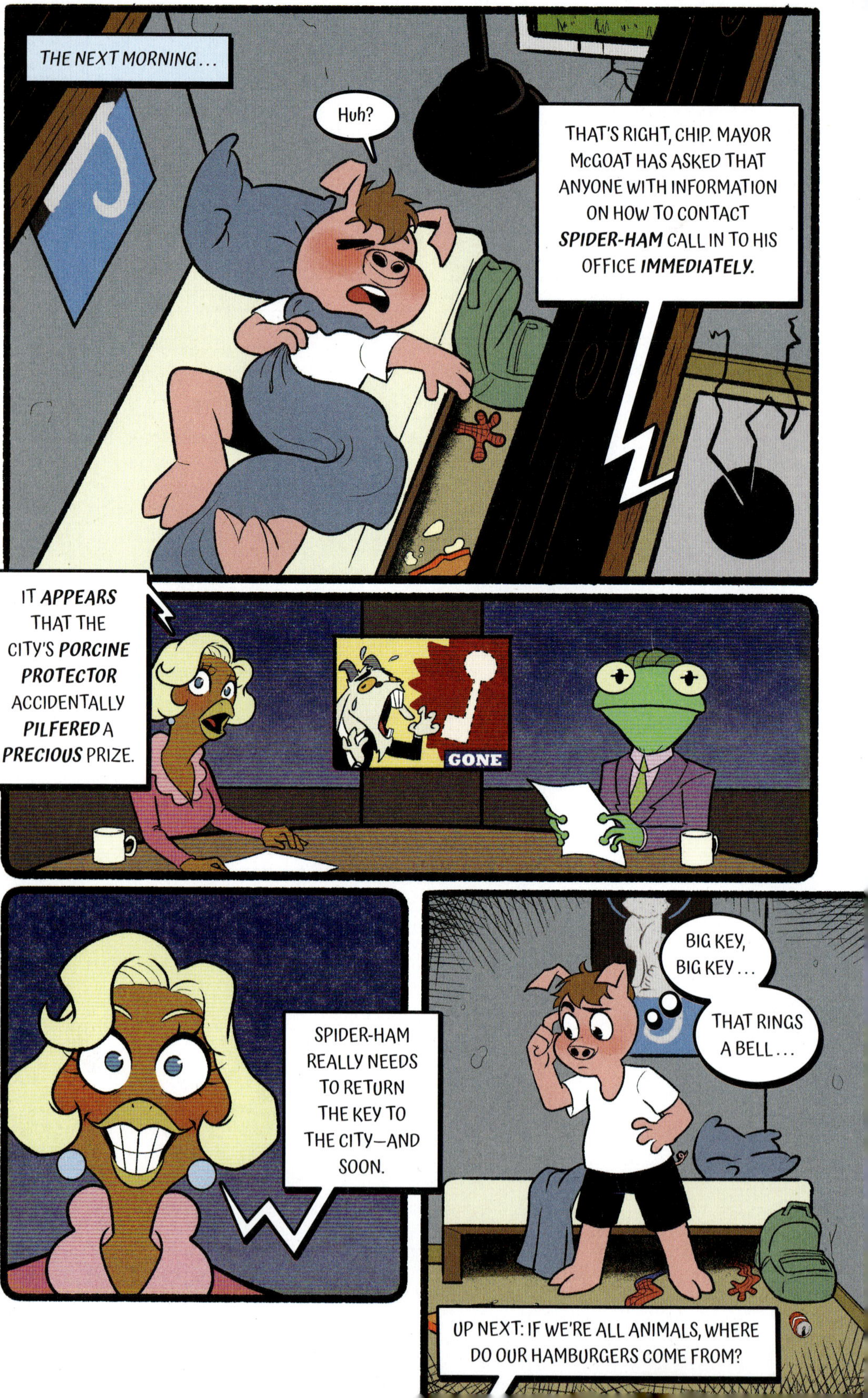
THE NEXT MORNING...
Huh?
THAT'S RIGHT, CHIP. MAYOR McGOAT HAS ASKED THAT ANYONE WITH INFORMATION ON HOW TO CONTACT SPIDER-HAM CALL IN TO HIS OFFICE IMMEDIATELY.
IT APPEARS THAT THE CITY'S PORCINE PROTECTOR ACCIDENTALLY PILFERED A PRECIOUS PRIZE.
GONE
SPIDER-HAM REALLY NEEDS TO RETURN THE KEY TO THE CITY—AND SOON.
BIG KEY, BIG KEY...
THAT RINGS A BELL...
UP NEXT: IF WE'RE ALL ANIMALS, WHERE DO OUR HAMBURGERS COME FROM?

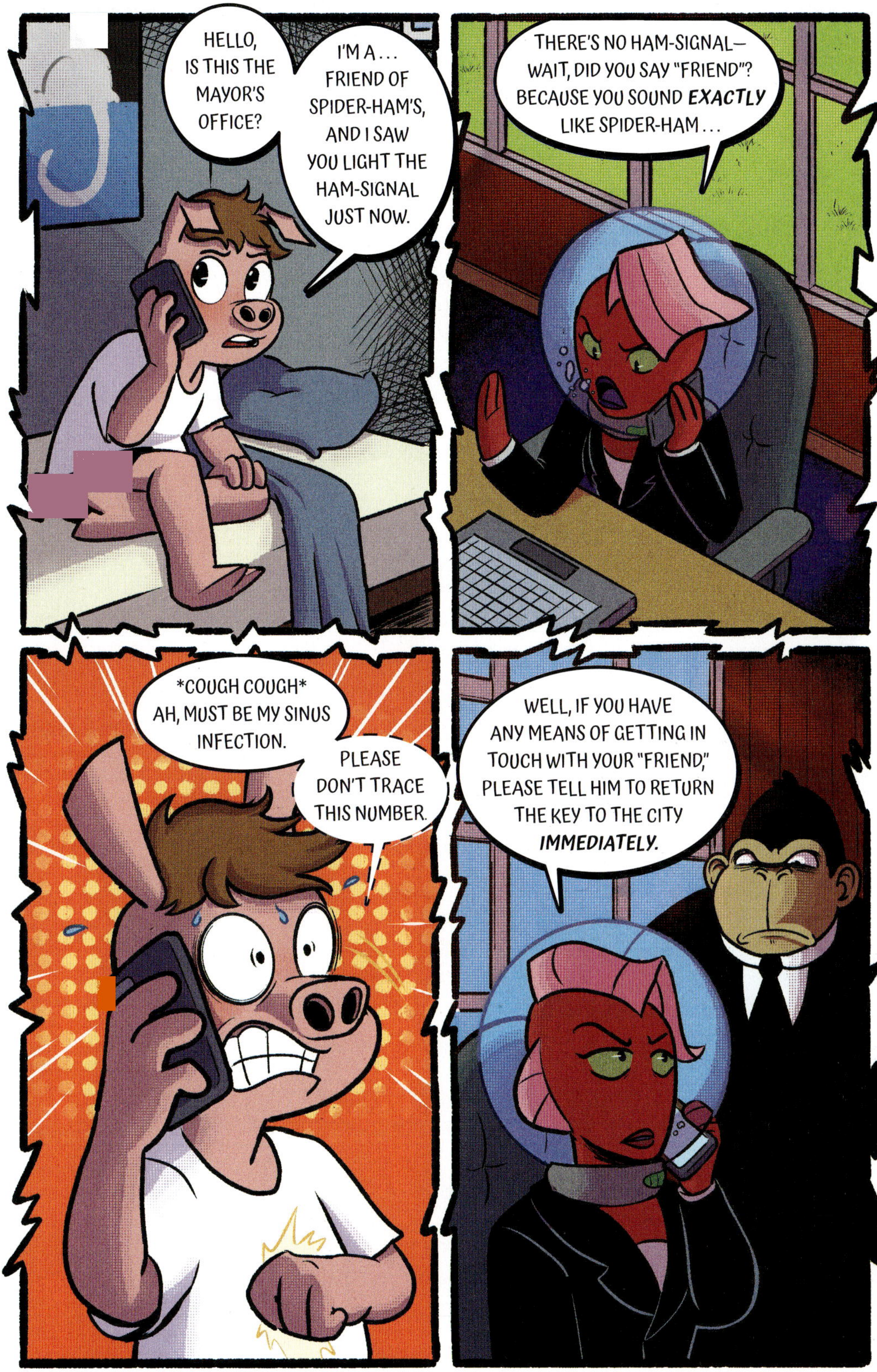
HELLO, IS THIS THE MAYOR'S OFFICE?
I'M A... FRIEND OF SPIDER-HAM'S, AND I SAW YOU LIGHT THE HAM-SIGNAL JUST NOW.
THERE'S NO HAM-SIGNAL— WAIT, DID YOU SAY "FRIEND"? BECAUSE YOU SOUND **EXACTLY** LIKE SPIDER-HAM...
COUGH COUGH AH, MUST BE MY SINUS INFECTION.
PLEASE DON'T TRACE THIS NUMBER.
WELL, IF YOU HAVE ANY MEANS OF GETTING IN TOUCH WITH YOUR "FRIEND," PLEASE TELL HIM TO RETURN THE KEY TO THE CITY **IMMEDIATELY.**

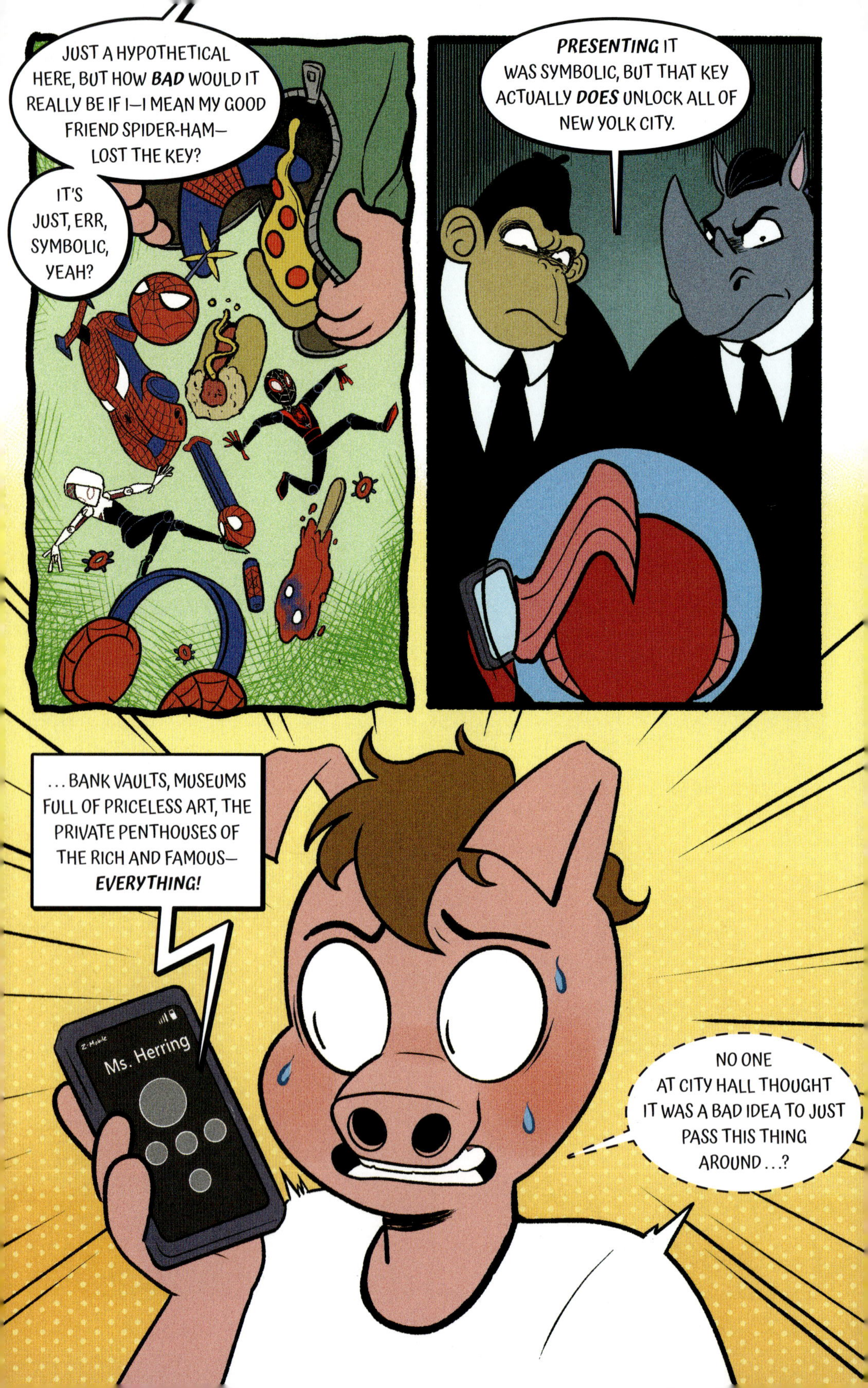
JUST A HYPOTHETICAL HERE, BUT HOW BAD WOULD IT REALLY BE IF I—I MEAN MY GOOD FRIEND SPIDER-HAM—LOST THE KEY?
IT'S JUST, ERR, SYMBOLIC, YEAH?
PRESENTING IT WAS SYMBOLIC, BUT THAT KEY ACTUALLY DOES UNLOCK ALL OF NEW YOLK CITY.
. . . BANK VAULTS, MUSEUMS FULL OF PRICELESS ART, THE PRIVATE PENTHOUSES OF THE RICH AND FAMOUS—EVERYTHING!
Ms. Herring
NO ONE AT CITY HALL THOUGHT IT WAS A BAD IDEA TO JUST PASS THIS THING AROUND . . .?

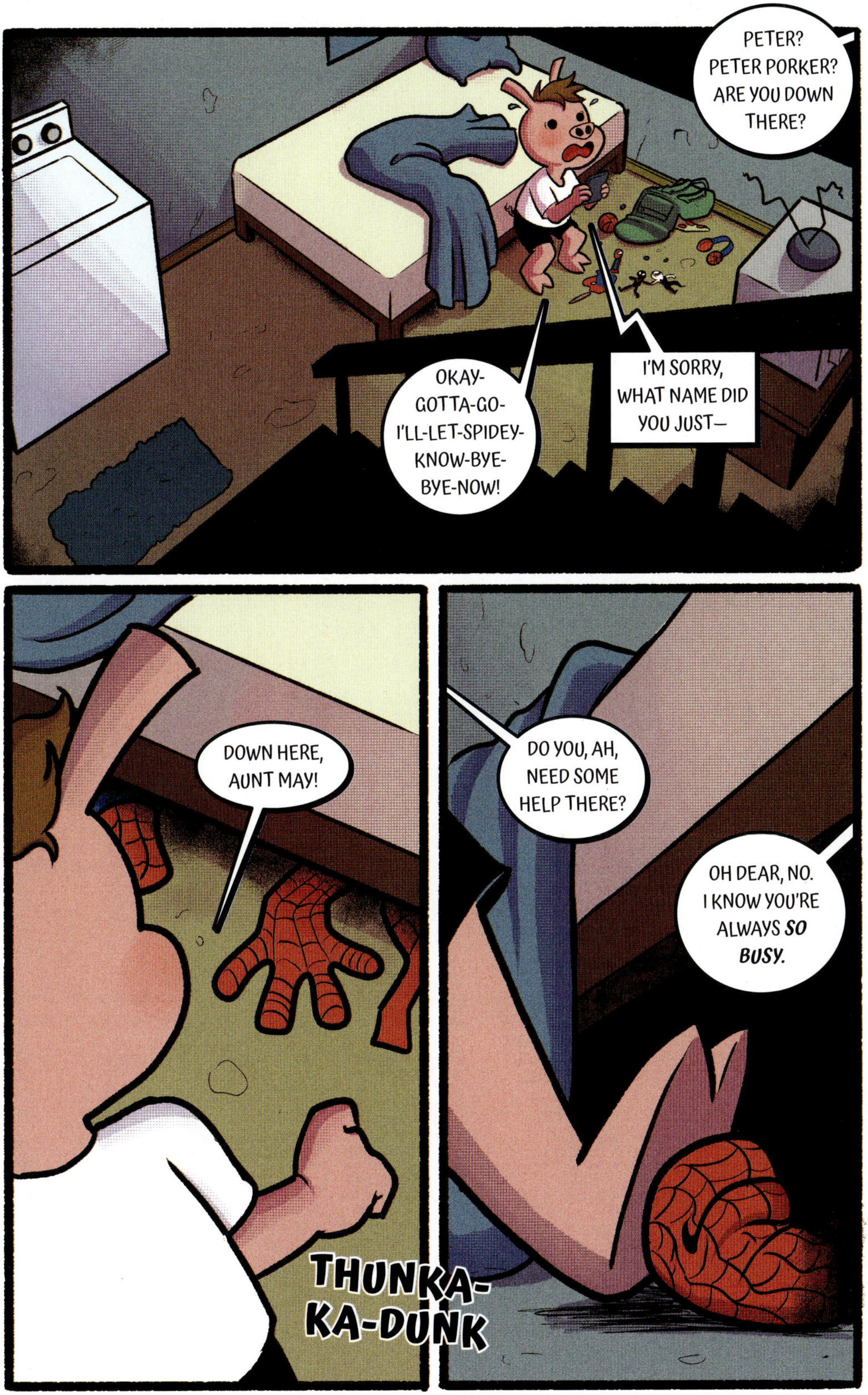
PETER? PETER PORKER? ARE YOU DOWN THERE?
OKAY-GOTTA-GO-I'LL-LET-SPIDEY-KNOW-BYE-BYE-NOW!
I'M SORRY, WHAT NAME DID YOU JUST—
DOWN HERE, AUNT MAY!
THUNKA-KA-DUNK
DO YOU, AH, NEED SOME HELP THERE?
OH DEAR, NO. I KNOW YOU'RE ALWAYS ***SO BUSY.***

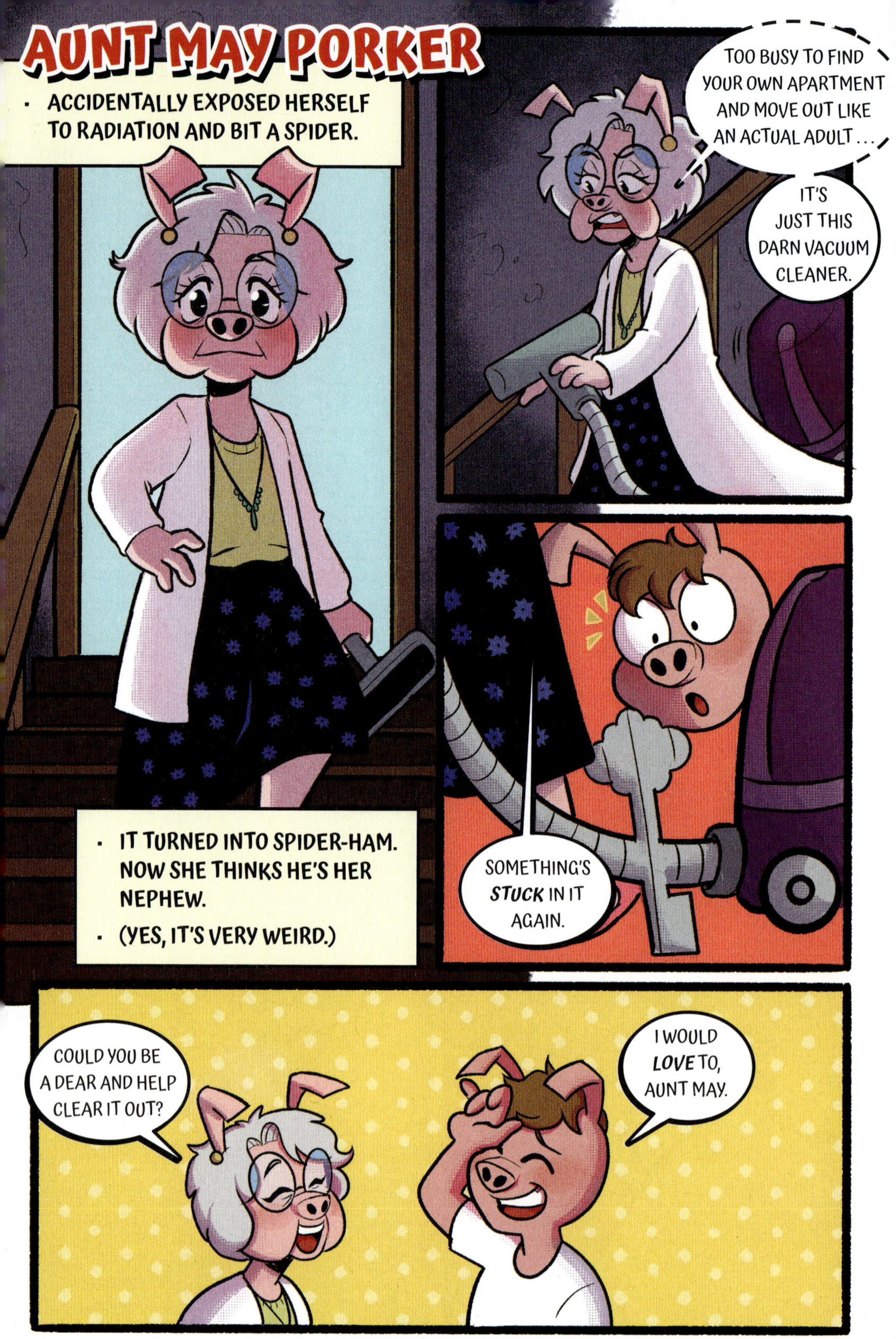
AUNT MAY PORKER
• ACCIDENTALLY EXPOSED HERSELF TO RADIATION AND BIT A SPIDER.
TOO BUSY TO FIND YOUR OWN APARTMENT AND MOVE OUT LIKE AN ACTUAL ADULT . . .
IT'S JUST THIS DARN VACUUM CLEANER.
• IT TURNED INTO SPIDER-HAM. NOW SHE THINKS HE'S HER NEPHEW.
• (YES, IT'S VERY WEIRD.)
SOMETHING'S STUCK IN IT AGAIN.
COULD YOU BE A DEAR AND HELP CLEAR IT OUT?
I WOULD LOVE TO, AUNT MAY.

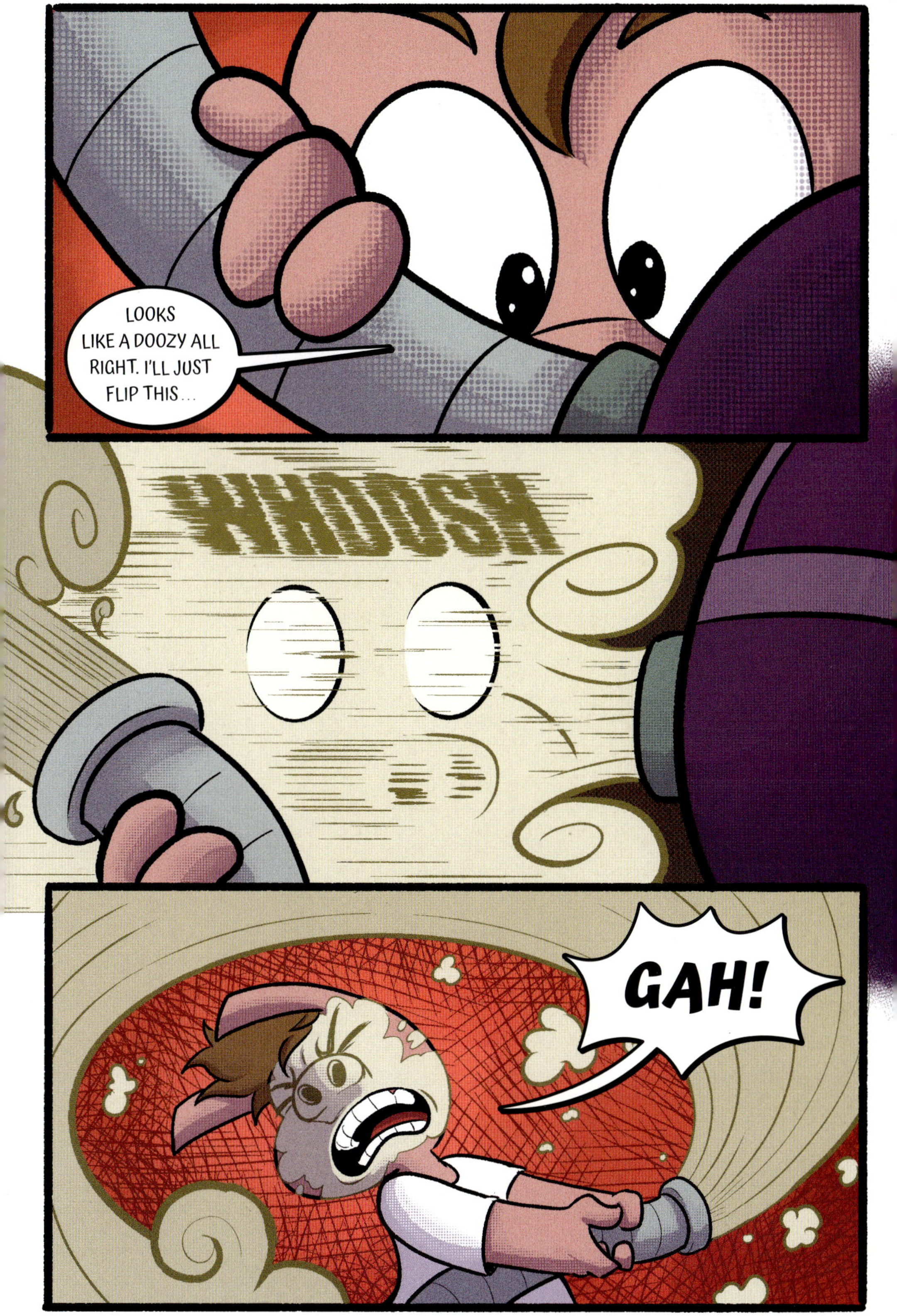
LOOKS LIKE A DOOZY ALL RIGHT. I'LL JUST FLIP THIS...
WHOOSH
GAH!

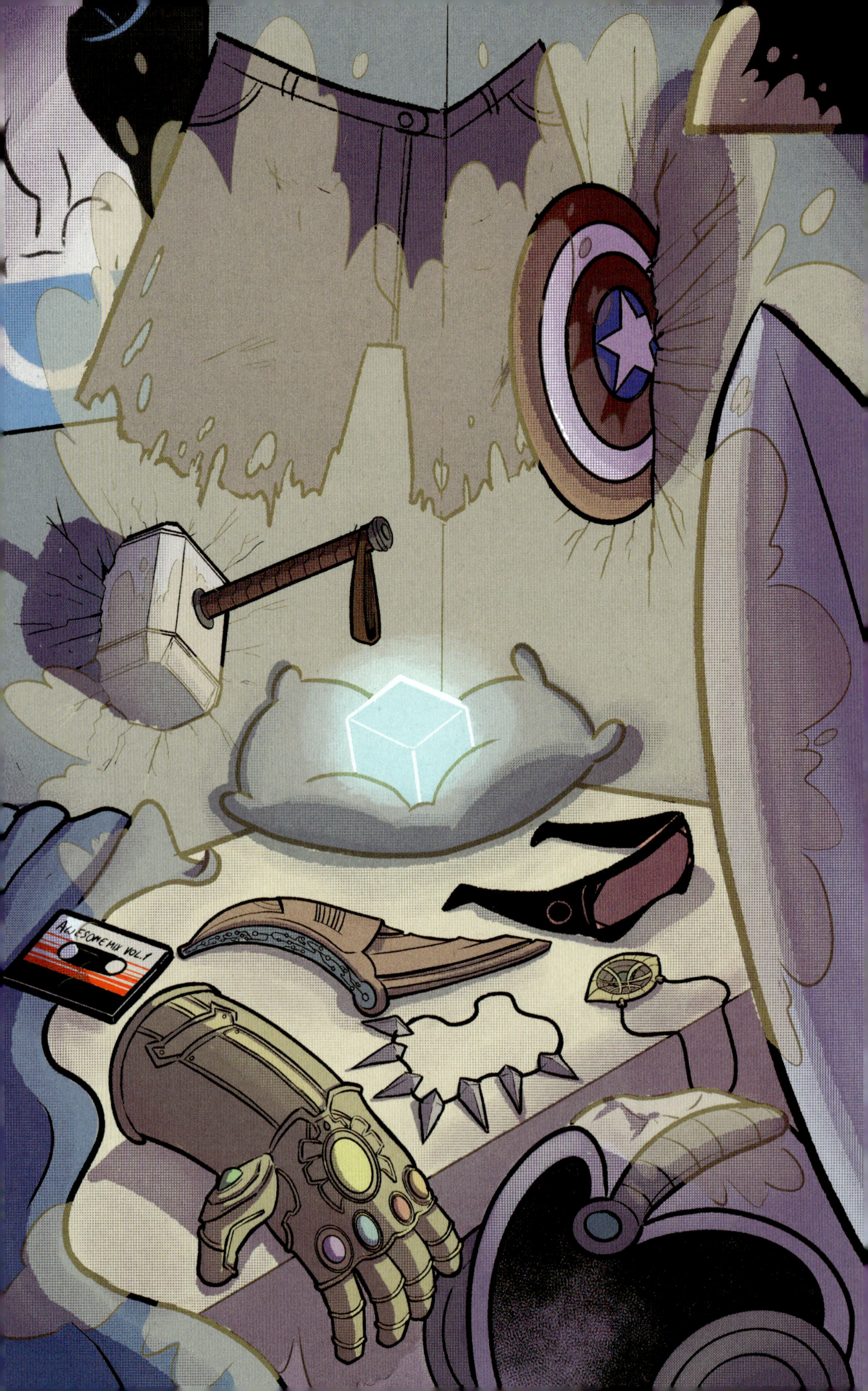
AWESOME MIX VOL.1

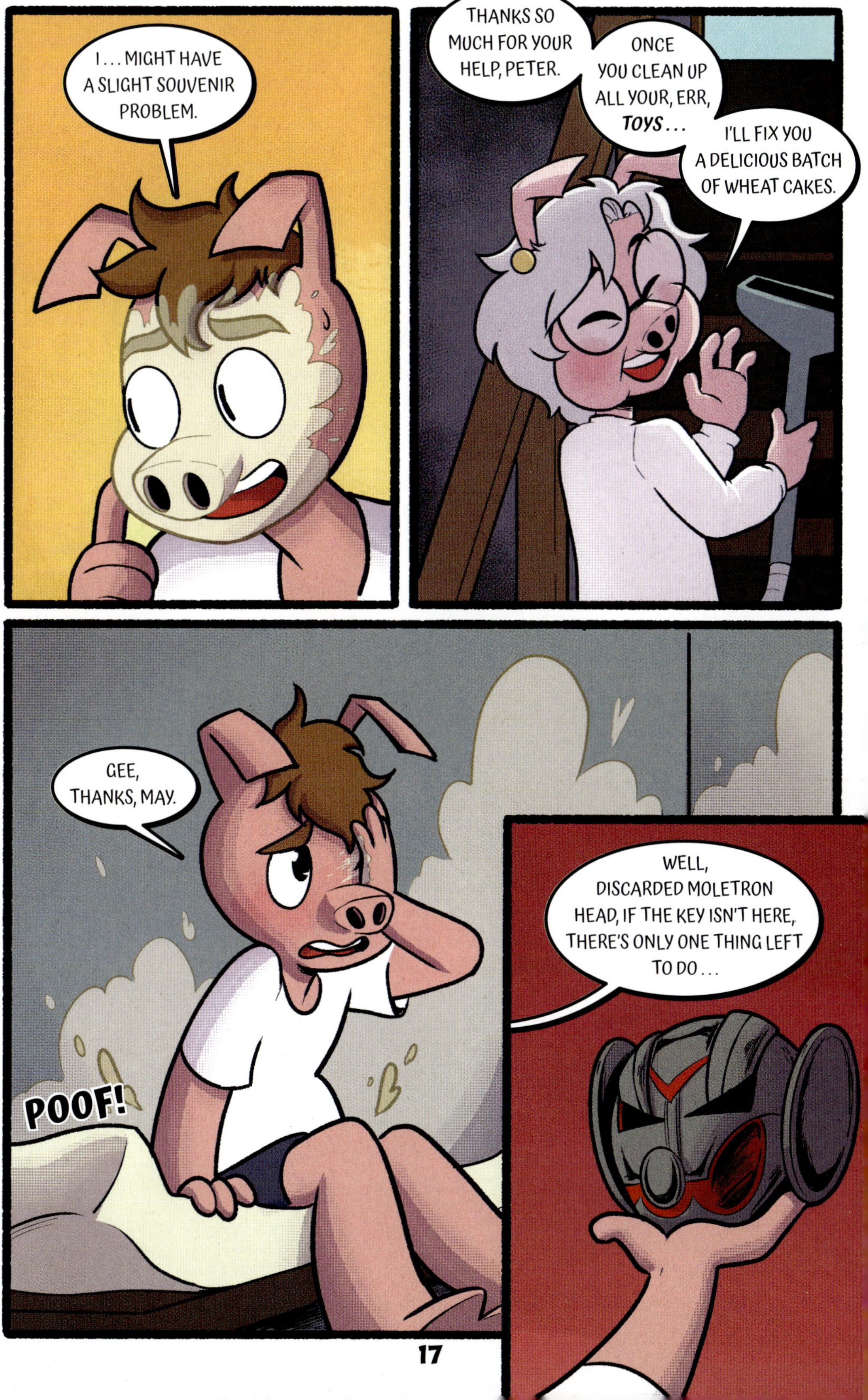
I . . . MIGHT HAVE A SLIGHT SOUVENIR PROBLEM.
THANKS SO MUCH FOR YOUR HELP, PETER.
ONCE YOU CLEAN UP ALL YOUR, ERR, TOYS . . .
I'LL FIX YOU A DELICIOUS BATCH OF WHEAT CAKES.
GEE, THANKS, MAY.
POOF!
WELL, DISCARDED MOLETRON HEAD, IF THE KEY ISN'T HERE, THERE'S ONLY ONE THING LEFT TO DO . . .

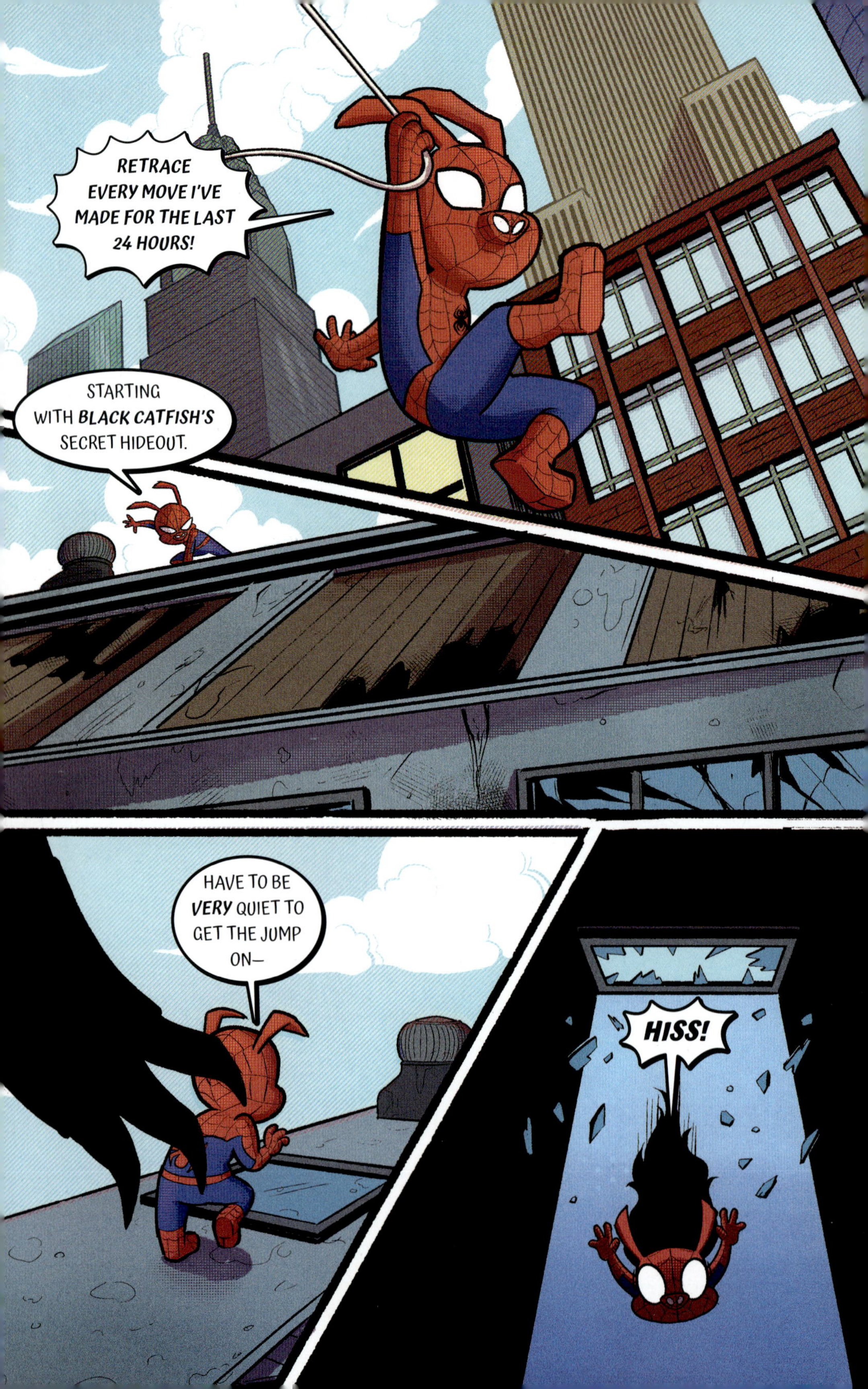
RETRACE EVERY MOVE I'VE MADE FOR THE LAST 24 HOURS!
STARTING WITH BLACK CATFISH'S SECRET HIDEOUT.
HAVE TO BE VERY QUIET TO GET THE JUMP ON—
HISS!

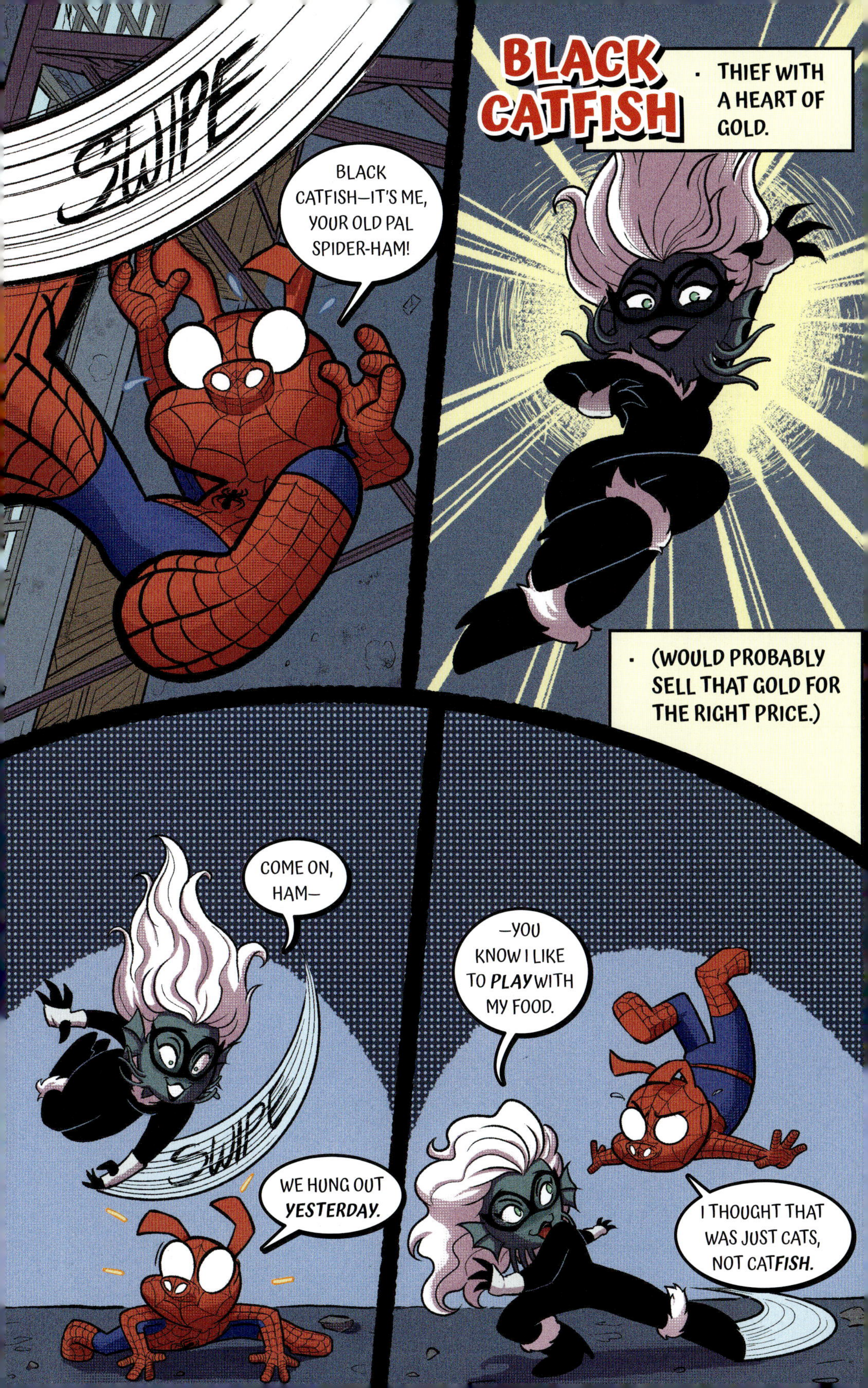
SWIPE
BLACK CATFISH—IT'S ME, YOUR OLD PAL SPIDER-HAM!
BLACK CATFISH
• THIEF WITH A HEART OF GOLD.
• (WOULD PROBABLY SELL THAT GOLD FOR THE RIGHT PRICE.)
COME ON, HAM—
SWIPE
WE HUNG OUT *YESTERDAY.*
—YOU KNOW I LIKE TO *PLAY* WITH MY FOOD.
I THOUGHT THAT WAS JUST CATS, NOT CAT*FISH.*

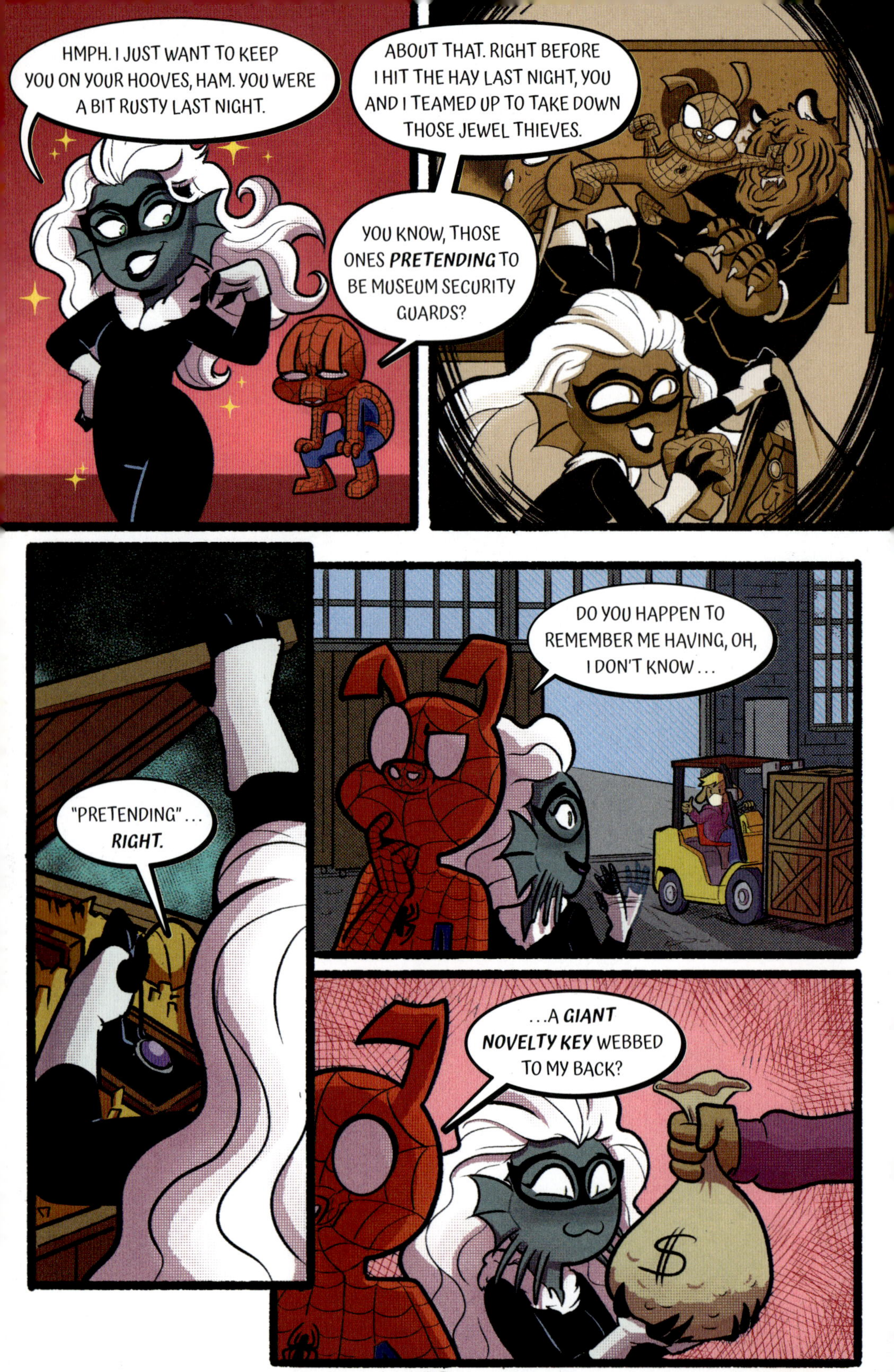
HMPH. I JUST WANT TO KEEP YOU ON YOUR HOOVES, HAM. YOU WERE A BIT RUSTY LAST NIGHT.
ABOUT THAT. RIGHT BEFORE I HIT THE HAY LAST NIGHT, YOU AND I TEAMED UP TO TAKE DOWN THOSE JEWEL THIEVES.
YOU KNOW, THOSE ONES ***PRETENDING*** TO BE MUSEUM SECURITY GUARDS?
"PRETENDING" . . . ***RIGHT.***
DO YOU HAPPEN TO REMEMBER ME HAVING, OH, I DON'T KNOW . . .
. . . A ***GIANT NOVELTY KEY*** WEBBED TO MY BACK?

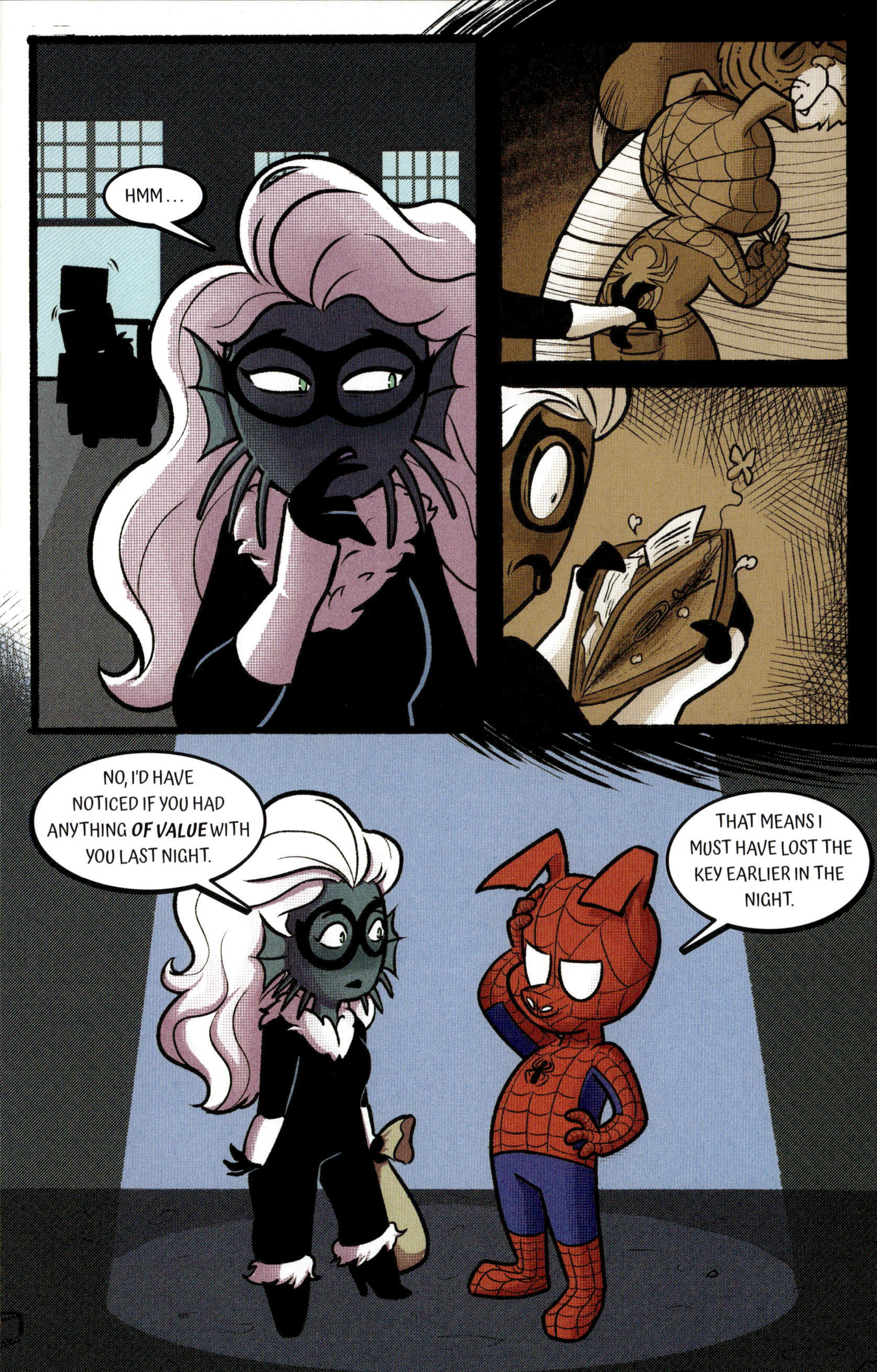
HMM...
NO, I'D HAVE NOTICED IF YOU HAD ANYTHING OF VALUE WITH YOU LAST NIGHT.
THAT MEANS I MUST HAVE LOST THE KEY EARLIER IN THE NIGHT.

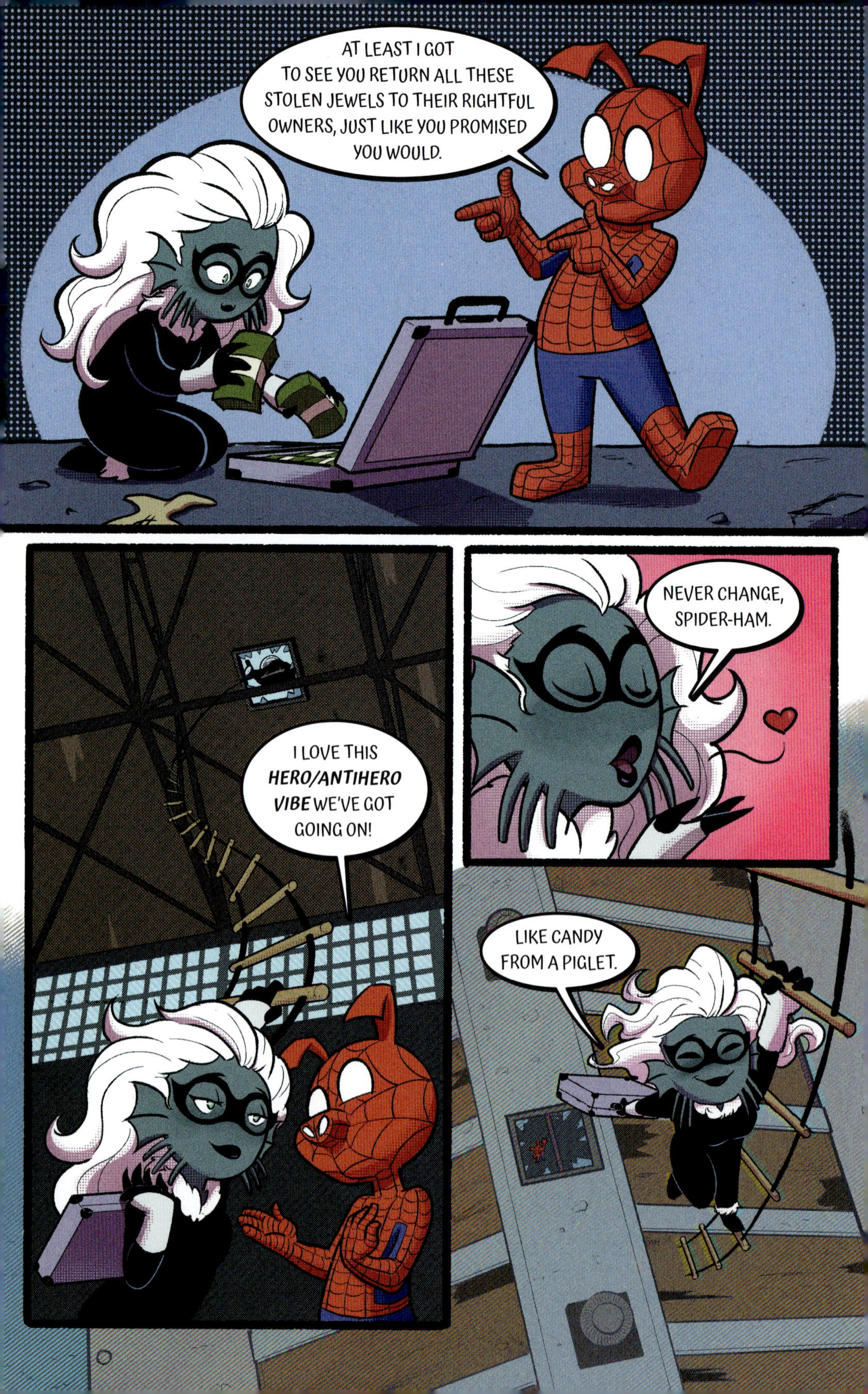
AT LEAST I GOT TO SEE YOU RETURN ALL THESE STOLEN JEWELS TO THEIR RIGHTFUL OWNERS, JUST LIKE YOU PROMISED YOU WOULD.
I LOVE THIS ***HERO/ANTIHERO VIBE*** WE'VE GOT GOING ON!
NEVER CHANGE, SPIDER-HAM.
LIKE CANDY FROM A PIGLET.

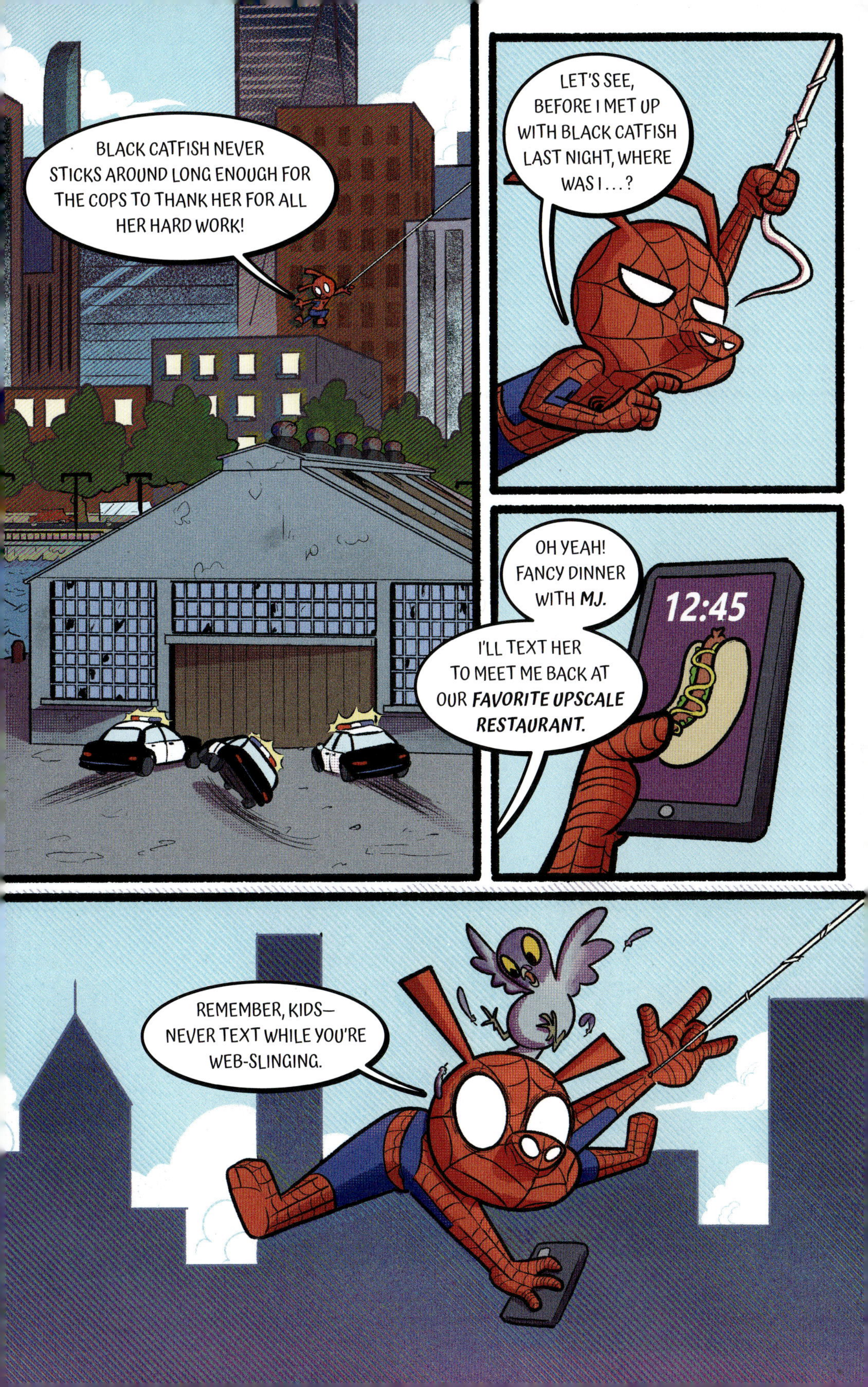
BLACK CATFISH NEVER STICKS AROUND LONG ENOUGH FOR THE COPS TO THANK HER FOR ALL HER HARD WORK!
LET'S SEE, BEFORE I MET UP WITH BLACK CATFISH LAST NIGHT, WHERE WAS I . . . ?
OH YEAH! FANCY DINNER WITH **MJ.**
12:45
I'LL TEXT HER TO MEET ME BACK AT OUR ***FAVORITE UPSCALE RESTAURANT.***
REMEMBER, KIDS— NEVER TEXT WHILE YOU'RE WEB-SLINGING.

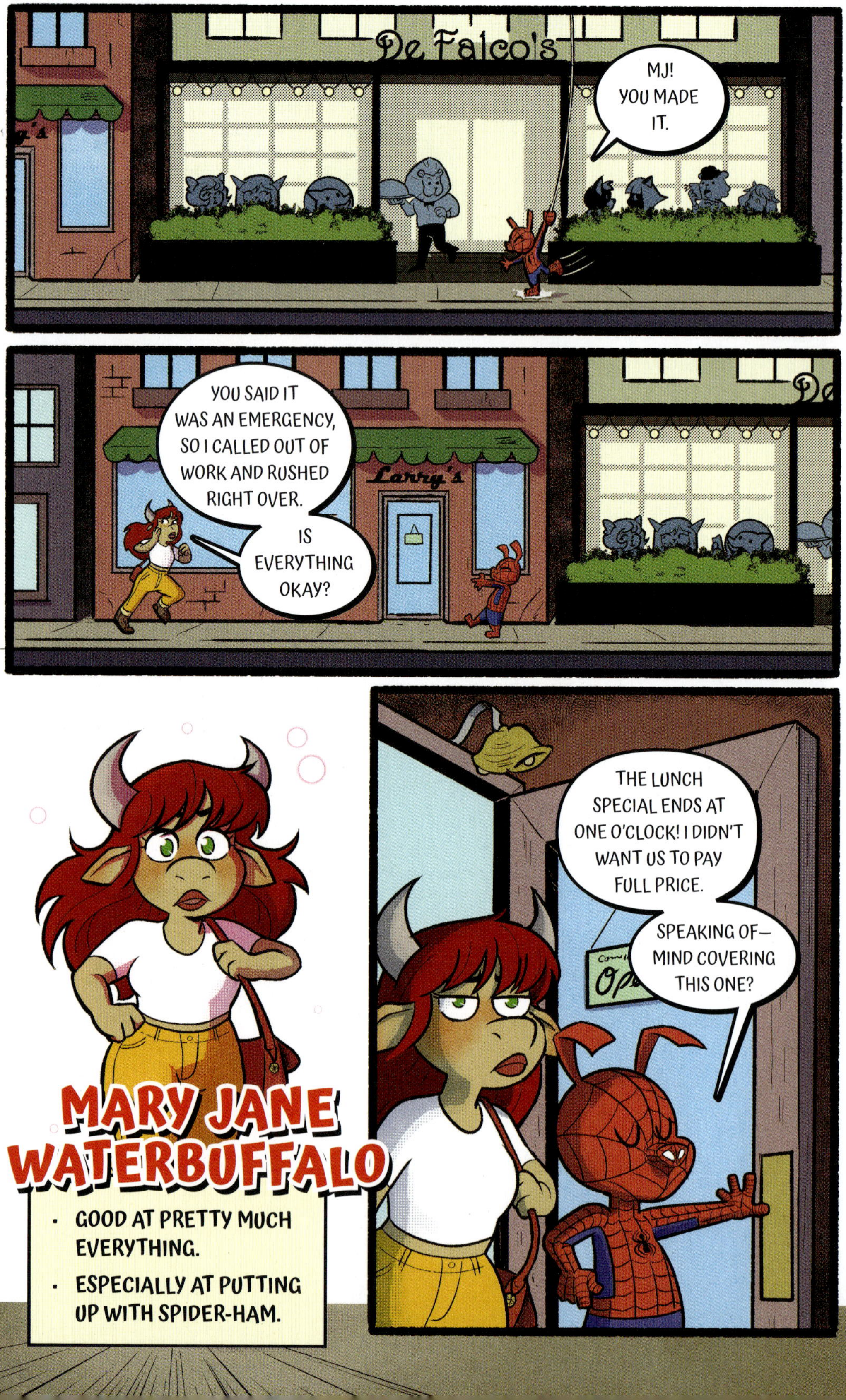
De Falco's
MJ! YOU MADE IT.
YOU SAID IT WAS AN EMERGENCY, SO I CALLED OUT OF WORK AND RUSHED RIGHT OVER.
IS EVERYTHING OKAY?
Larry's
THE LUNCH SPECIAL ENDS AT ONE O'CLOCK! I DIDN'T WANT US TO PAY FULL PRICE.
SPEAKING OF— MIND COVERING THIS ONE?
MARY JANE WATERBUFFALO
• GOOD AT PRETTY MUCH EVERYTHING.
• ESPECIALLY AT PUTTING UP WITH SPIDER-HAM.

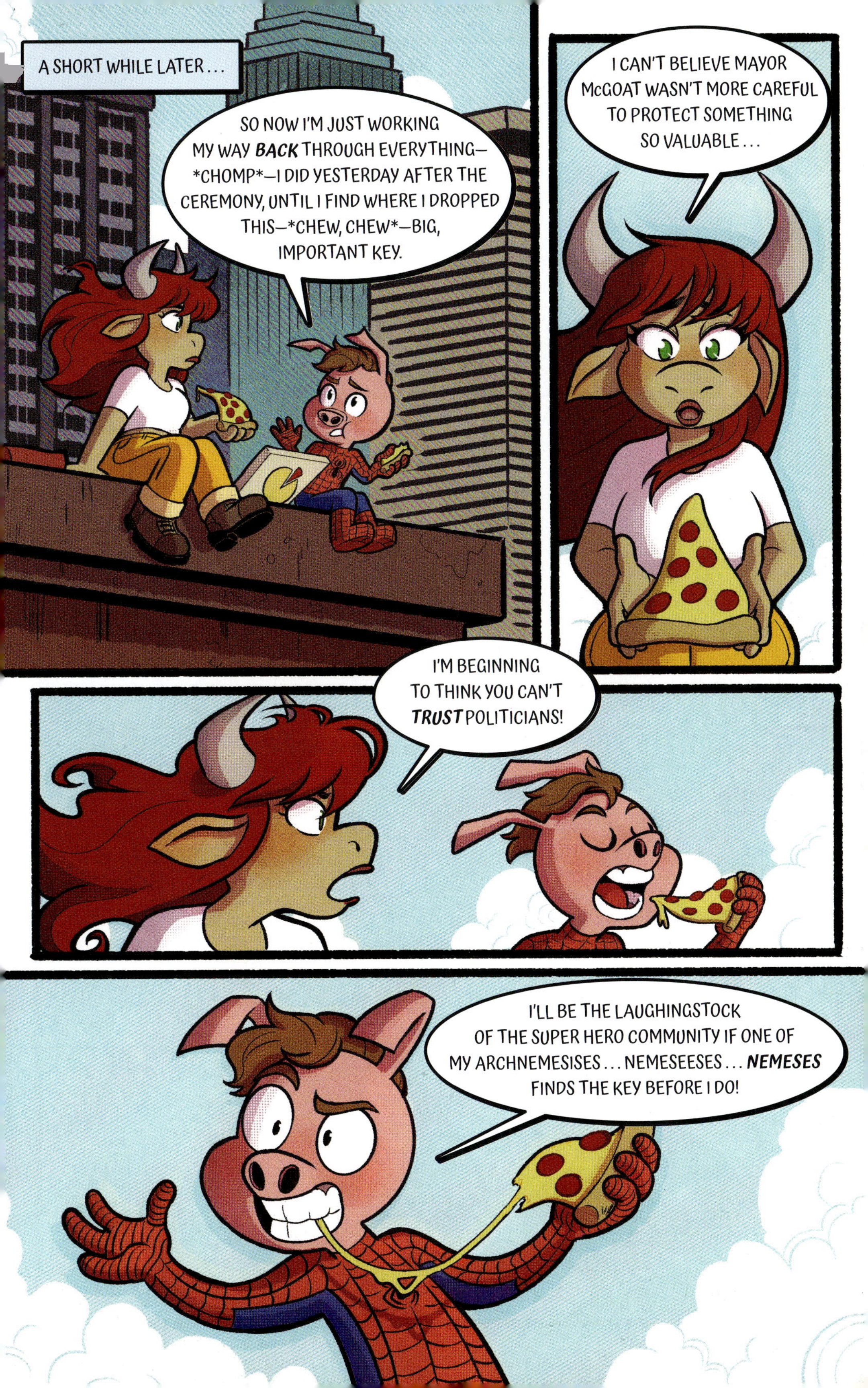
A SHORT WHILE LATER . . .
SO NOW I'M JUST WORKING MY WAY BACK THROUGH EVERYTHING—*CHOMP*—I DID YESTERDAY AFTER THE CEREMONY, UNTIL I FIND WHERE I DROPPED THIS—*CHEW, CHEW*—BIG, IMPORTANT KEY.
I CAN'T BELIEVE MAYOR McGOAT WASN'T MORE CAREFUL TO PROTECT SOMETHING SO VALUABLE . . .
I'M BEGINNING TO THINK YOU CAN'T TRUST POLITICIANS!
I'LL BE THE LAUGHINGSTOCK OF THE SUPER HERO COMMUNITY IF ONE OF MY ARCHNEMESISES . . . NEMESEESES . . . NEMESES FINDS THE KEY BEFORE I DO!

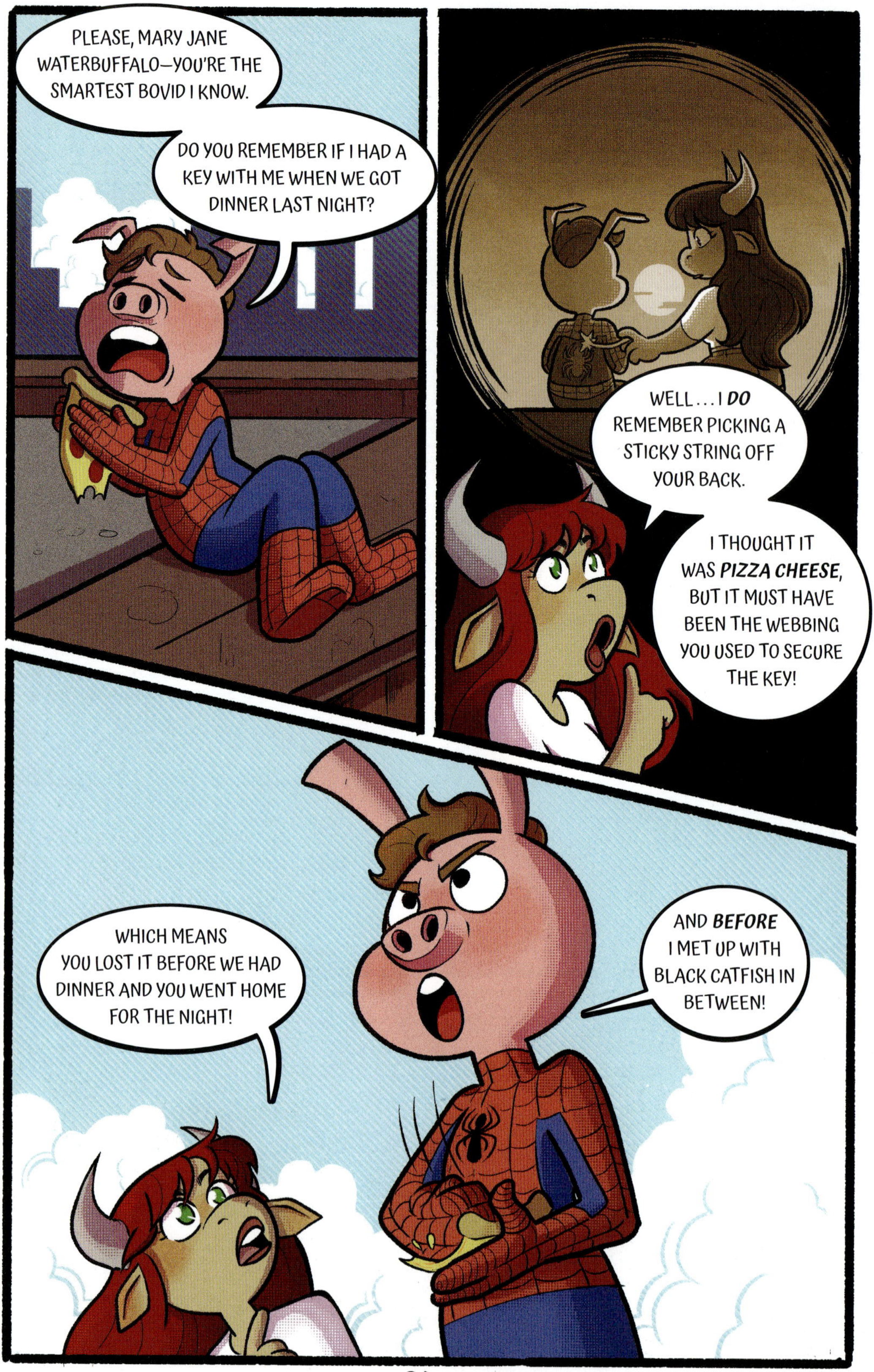
PLEASE, MARY JANE WATERBUFFALO—YOU'RE THE SMARTEST BOVID I KNOW.
DO YOU REMEMBER IF I HAD A KEY WITH ME WHEN WE GOT DINNER LAST NIGHT?
WELL . . . I **DO** REMEMBER PICKING A STICKY STRING OFF YOUR BACK.
I THOUGHT IT WAS **PIZZA CHEESE**, BUT IT MUST HAVE BEEN THE WEBBING YOU USED TO SECURE THE KEY!
WHICH MEANS YOU LOST IT BEFORE WE HAD DINNER AND YOU WENT HOME FOR THE NIGHT!
AND **BEFORE** I MET UP WITH BLACK CATFISH IN BETWEEN!

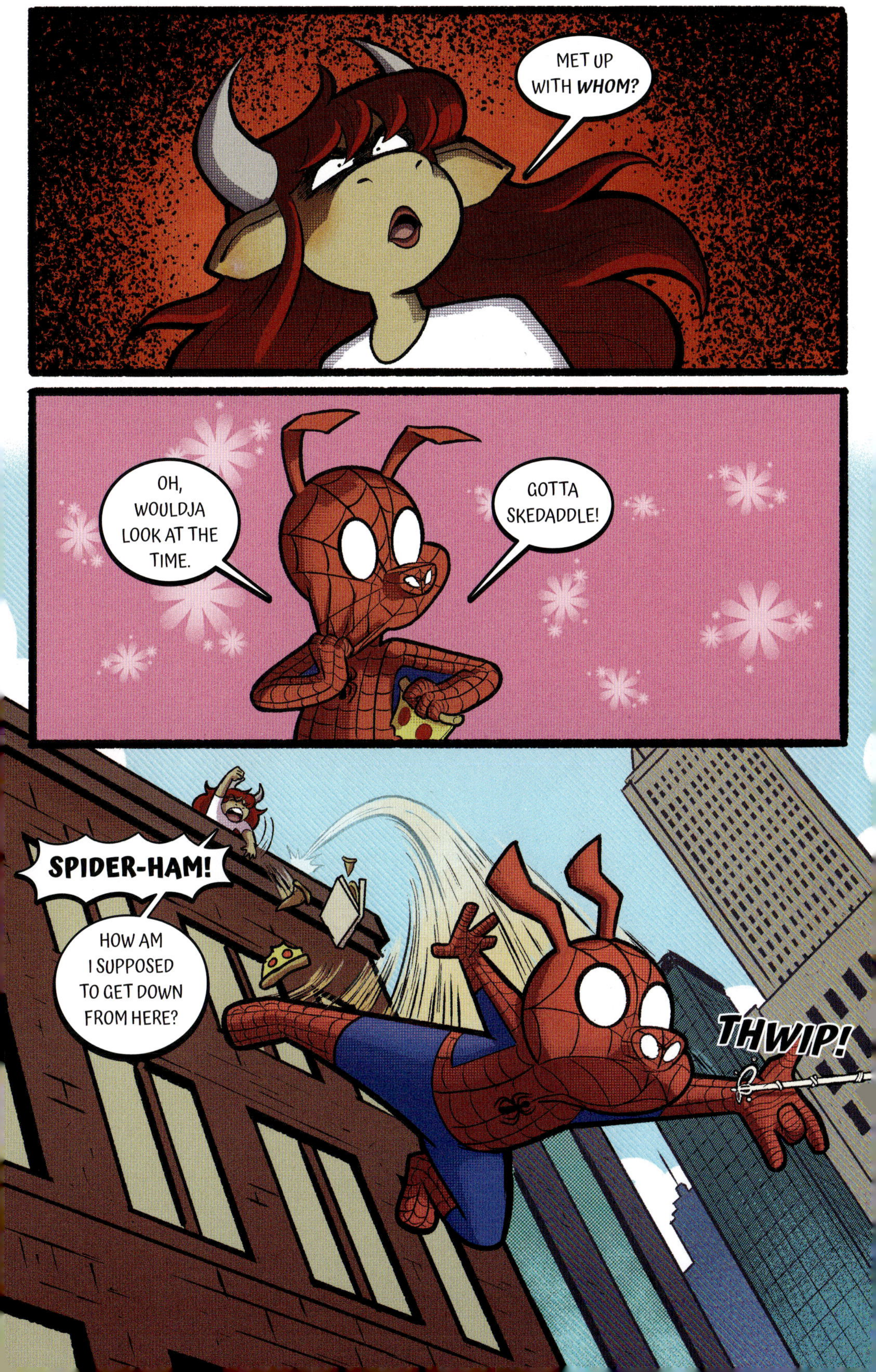

MET UP WITH **WHOM?**
OH, WOULDJA LOOK AT THE TIME.
GOTTA SKEDADDLE!
SPIDER-HAM!
HOW AM I SUPPOSED TO GET DOWN FROM HERE?
THWIP!

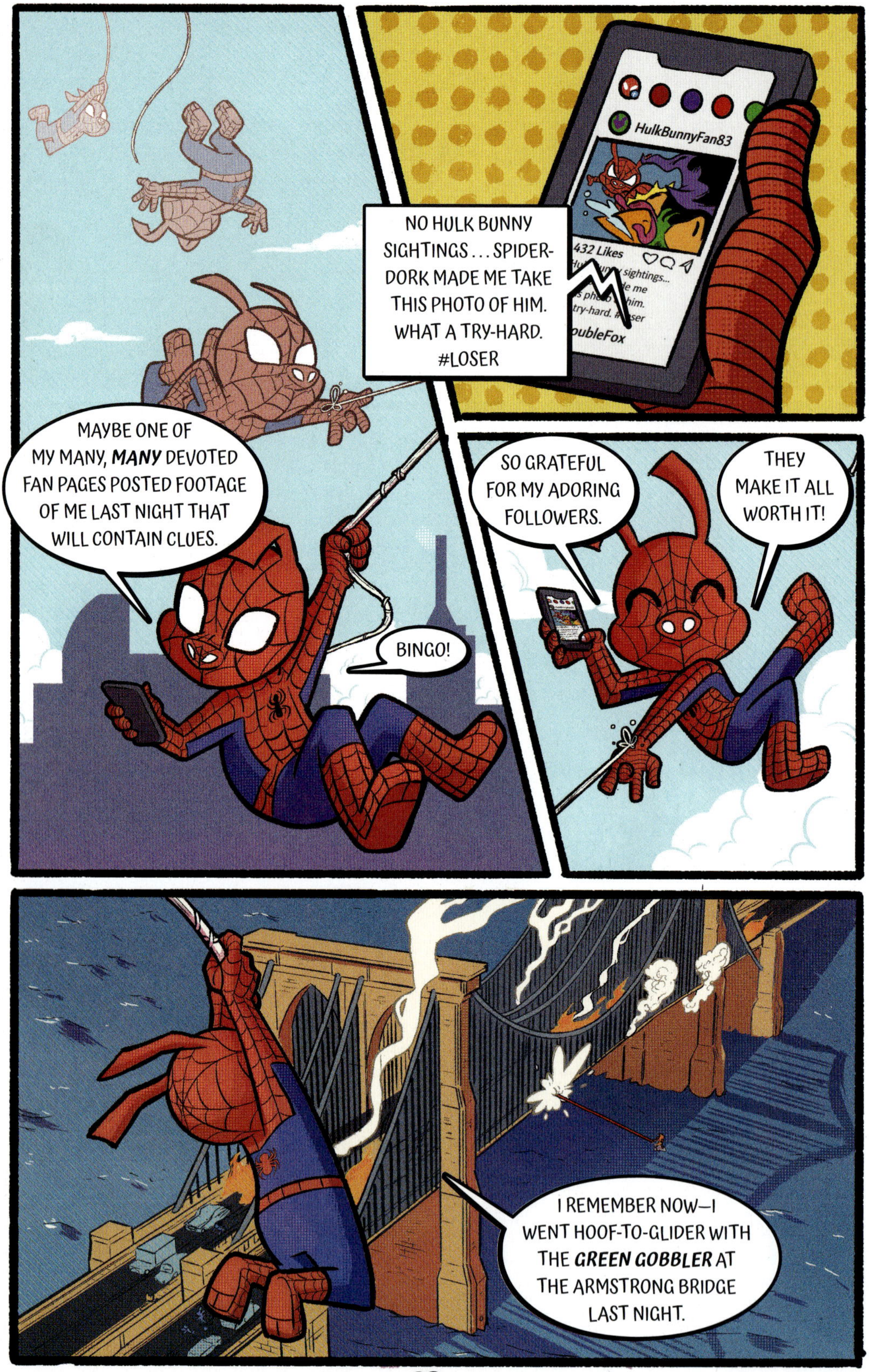
MAYBE ONE OF MY MANY, ***MANY*** DEVOTED FAN PAGES POSTED FOOTAGE OF ME LAST NIGHT THAT WILL CONTAIN CLUES.
BINGO!
HulkBunnyFan83
432 Likes
NO HULK BUNNY SIGHTINGS . . . SPIDER-DORK MADE ME TAKE THIS PHOTO OF HIM. WHAT A TRY-HARD. #LOSER
SO GRATEFUL FOR MY ADORING FOLLOWERS.
THEY MAKE IT ALL WORTH IT!
I REMEMBER NOW—I WENT HOOF-TO-GLIDER WITH THE ***GREEN GOBBLER*** AT THE ARMSTRONG BRIDGE LAST NIGHT.

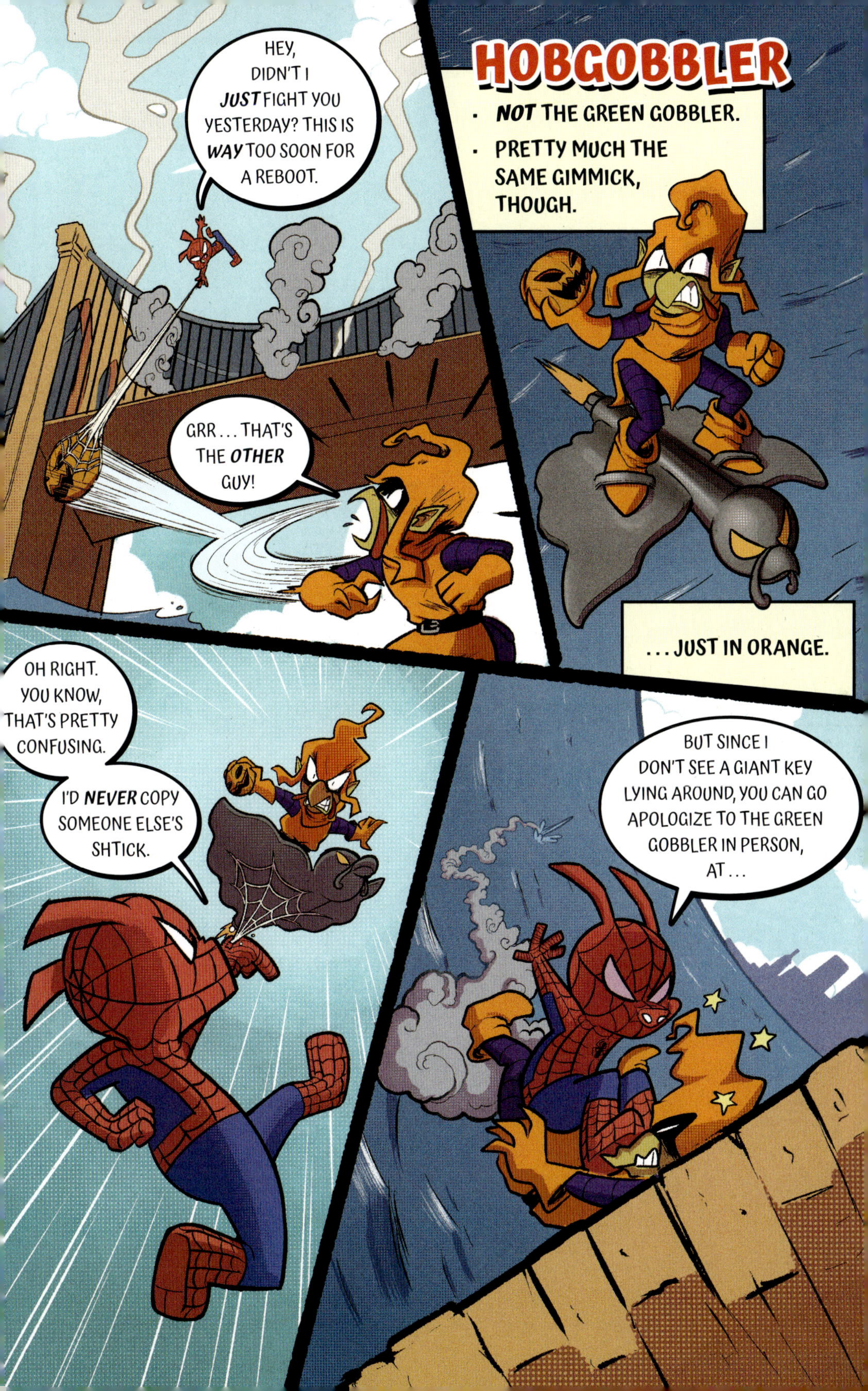
HEY, DIDN'T I JUST FIGHT YOU YESTERDAY? THIS IS WAY TOO SOON FOR A REBOOT.
GRR . . . THAT'S THE OTHER GUY!
HOBGOBBLER
· NOT THE GREEN GOBBLER.
· PRETTY MUCH THE SAME GIMMICK, THOUGH.
. . . JUST IN ORANGE.
OH RIGHT. YOU KNOW, THAT'S PRETTY CONFUSING.
I'D NEVER COPY SOMEONE ELSE'S SHTICK.
BUT SINCE I DON'T SEE A GIANT KEY LYING AROUND, YOU CAN GO APOLOGIZE TO THE GREEN GOBBLER IN PERSON, AT . . .

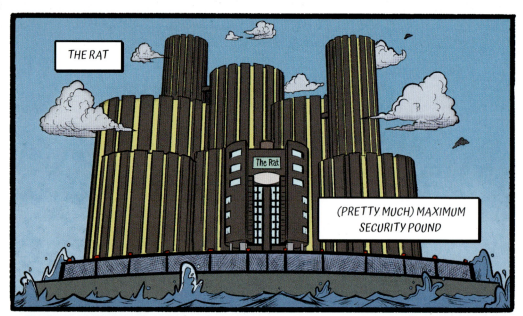

THE RAT

(PRETTY MUCH) MAXIMUM SECURITY POUND

WHAT DO YOU *MEAN* THE GREEN GOBBLER IS LOOSE AGAIN?

HE'S ONE OF MY *MOST NOTORIOUS* FOES!

I JUST DROPPED HIM OFF *LAST NIGHT!*

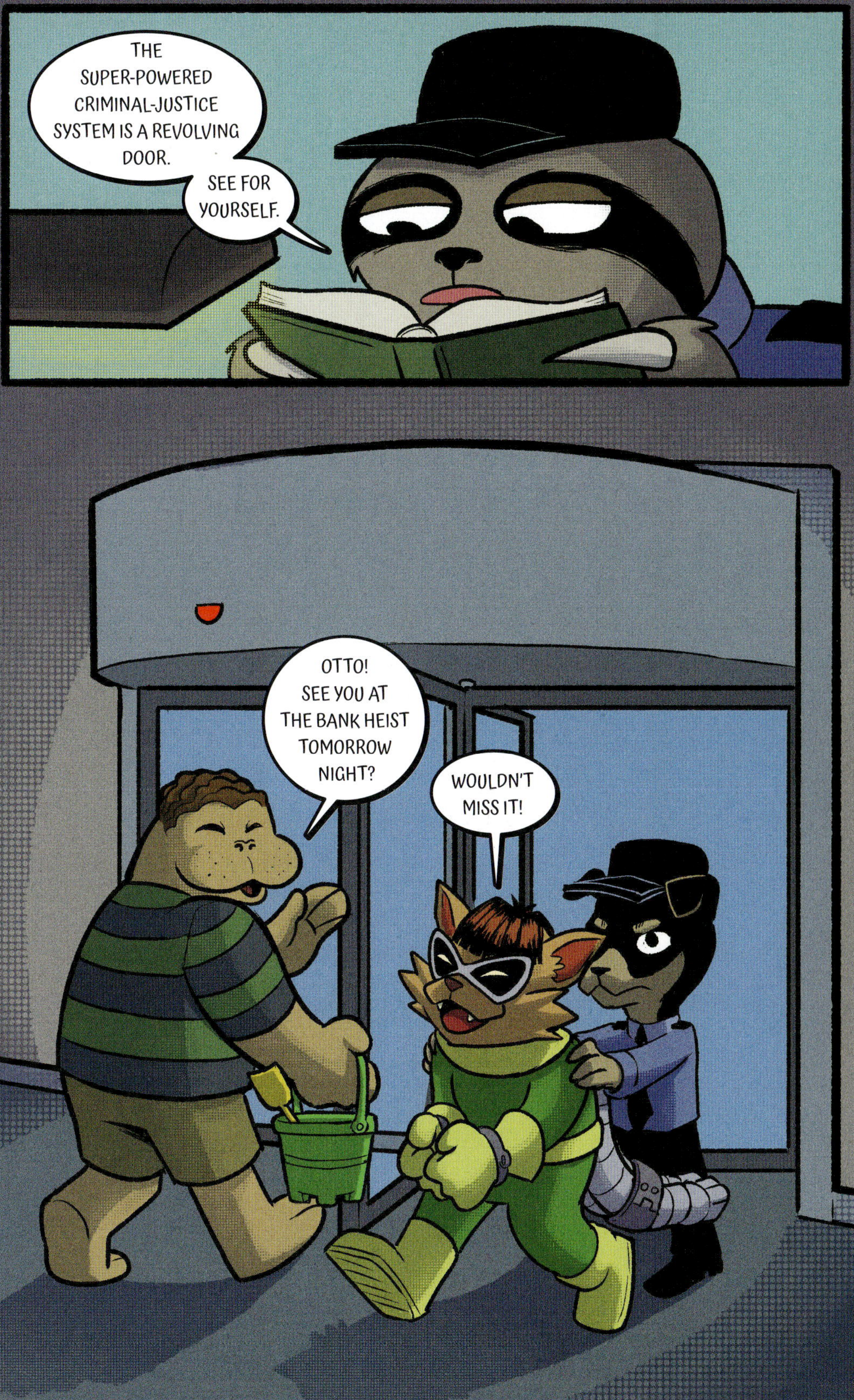
THE SUPER-POWERED CRIMINAL-JUSTICE SYSTEM IS A REVOLVING DOOR.
SEE FOR YOURSELF.
OTTO! SEE YOU AT THE BANK HEIST TOMORROW NIGHT?
WOULDN'T MISS IT!

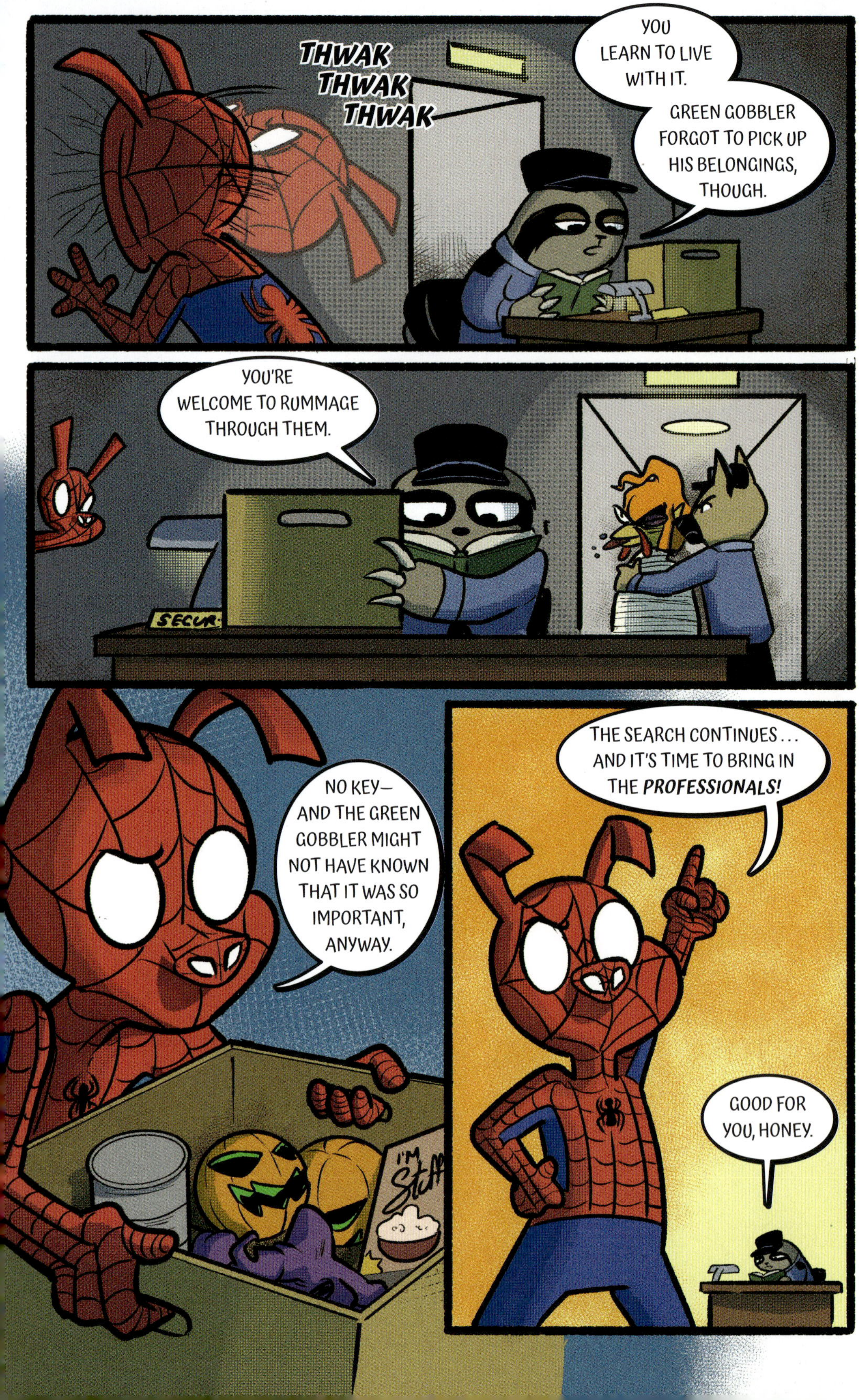
THWAK
THWAK
THWAK
YOU LEARN TO LIVE WITH IT.
GREEN GOBBLER FORGOT TO PICK UP HIS BELONGINGS, THOUGH.
YOU'RE WELCOME TO RUMMAGE THROUGH THEM.
SECUR
NO KEY— AND THE GREEN GOBBLER MIGHT NOT HAVE KNOWN THAT IT WAS SO IMPORTANT, ANYWAY.
THE SEARCH CONTINUES . . . AND IT'S TIME TO BRING IN THE ***PROFESSIONALS!***
GOOD FOR YOU, HONEY.

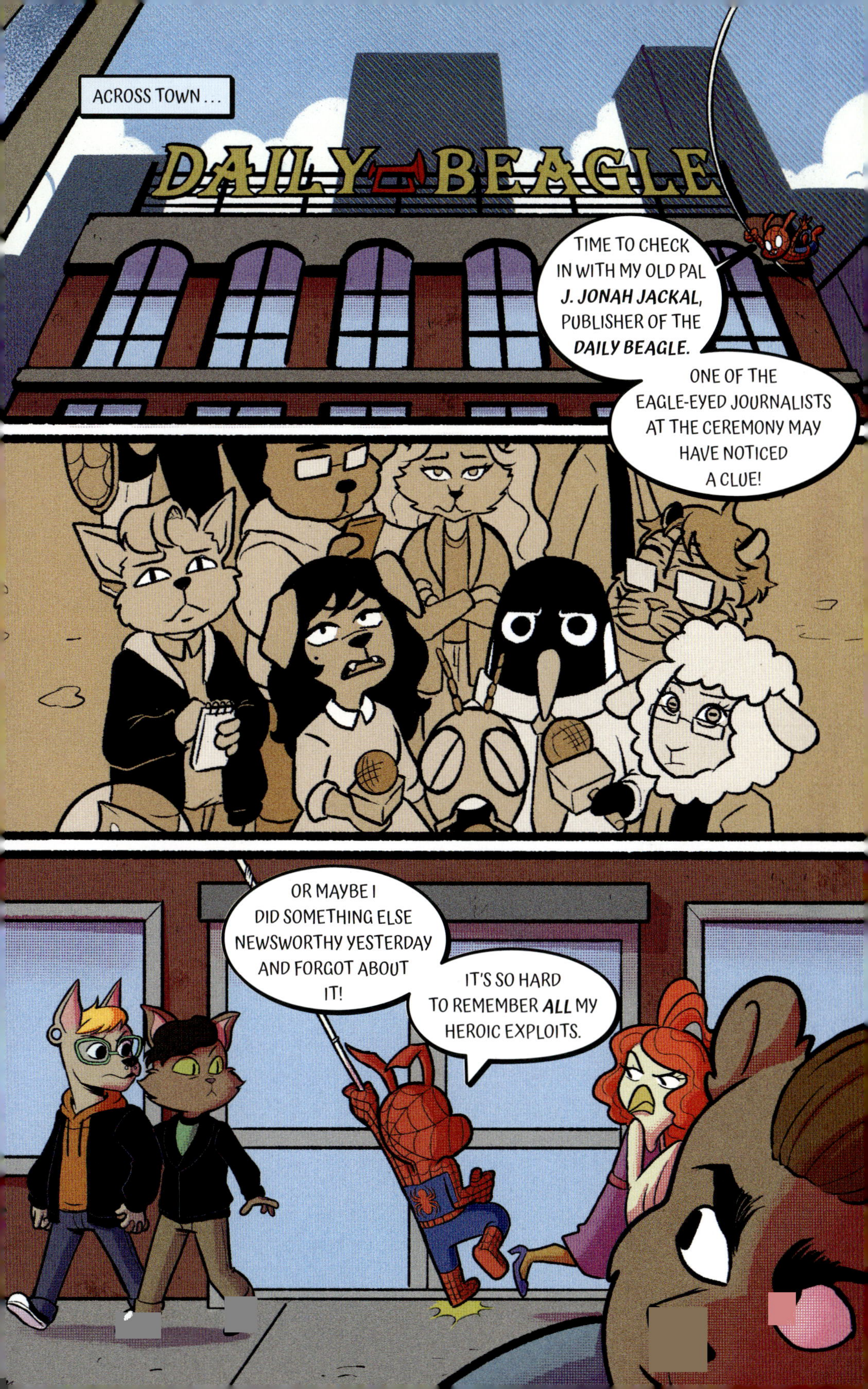
ACROSS TOWN . . .
DAILY BEAGLE
TIME TO CHECK IN WITH MY OLD PAL **J. JONAH JACKAL,** PUBLISHER OF THE ***DAILY BEAGLE.***
ONE OF THE EAGLE-EYED JOURNALISTS AT THE CEREMONY MAY HAVE NOTICED A CLUE!
OR MAYBE I DID SOMETHING ELSE NEWSWORTHY YESTERDAY AND FORGOT ABOUT IT!
IT'S SO HARD TO REMEMBER ***ALL*** MY HEROIC EXPLOITS.

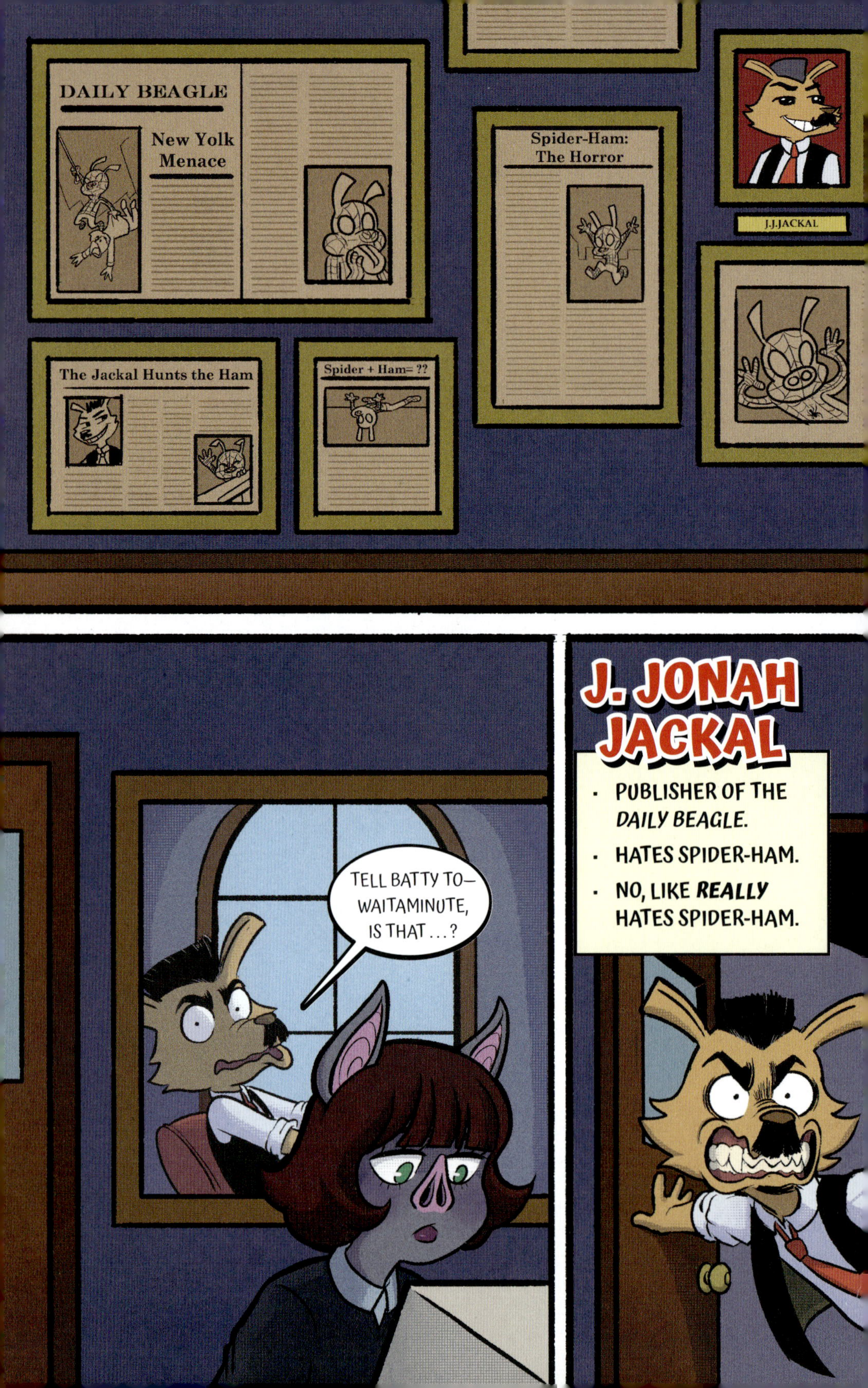
DAILY BEAGLE
New Yolk Menace
Spider-Ham: The Horror
J.J.JACKAL
The Jackal Hunts the Ham
Spider + Ham= ??
TELL BATTY TO— WAITAMINUTE, IS THAT . . . ?
J. JONAH JACKAL
· PUBLISHER OF THE *DAILY BEAGLE*.
· HATES SPIDER-HAM.
· NO, LIKE ***REALLY*** HATES SPIDER-HAM.

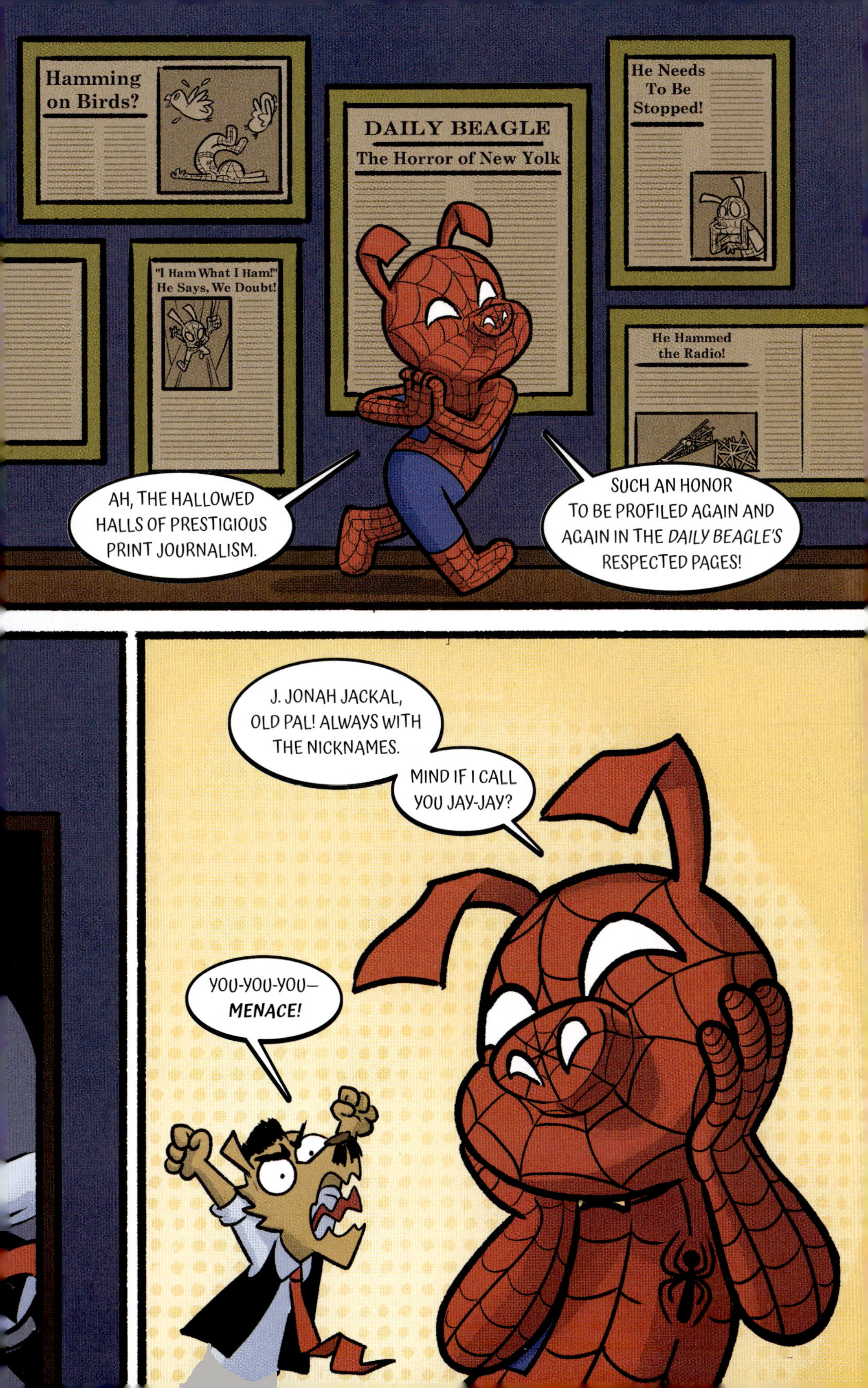
Hamming on Birds?
DAILY BEAGLE
The Horror of New Yolk
He Needs To Be Stopped!
"I Ham What I Ham!" He Says, We Doubt!
He Hammed the Radio!
AH, THE HALLOWED HALLS OF PRESTIGIOUS PRINT JOURNALISM.
SUCH AN HONOR TO BE PROFILED AGAIN AND AGAIN IN THE *DAILY BEAGLE'S* RESPECTED PAGES!
J. JONAH JACKAL, OLD PAL! ALWAYS WITH THE NICKNAMES.
MIND IF I CALL YOU JAY-JAY?
YOU-YOU-YOU— ***MENACE!***

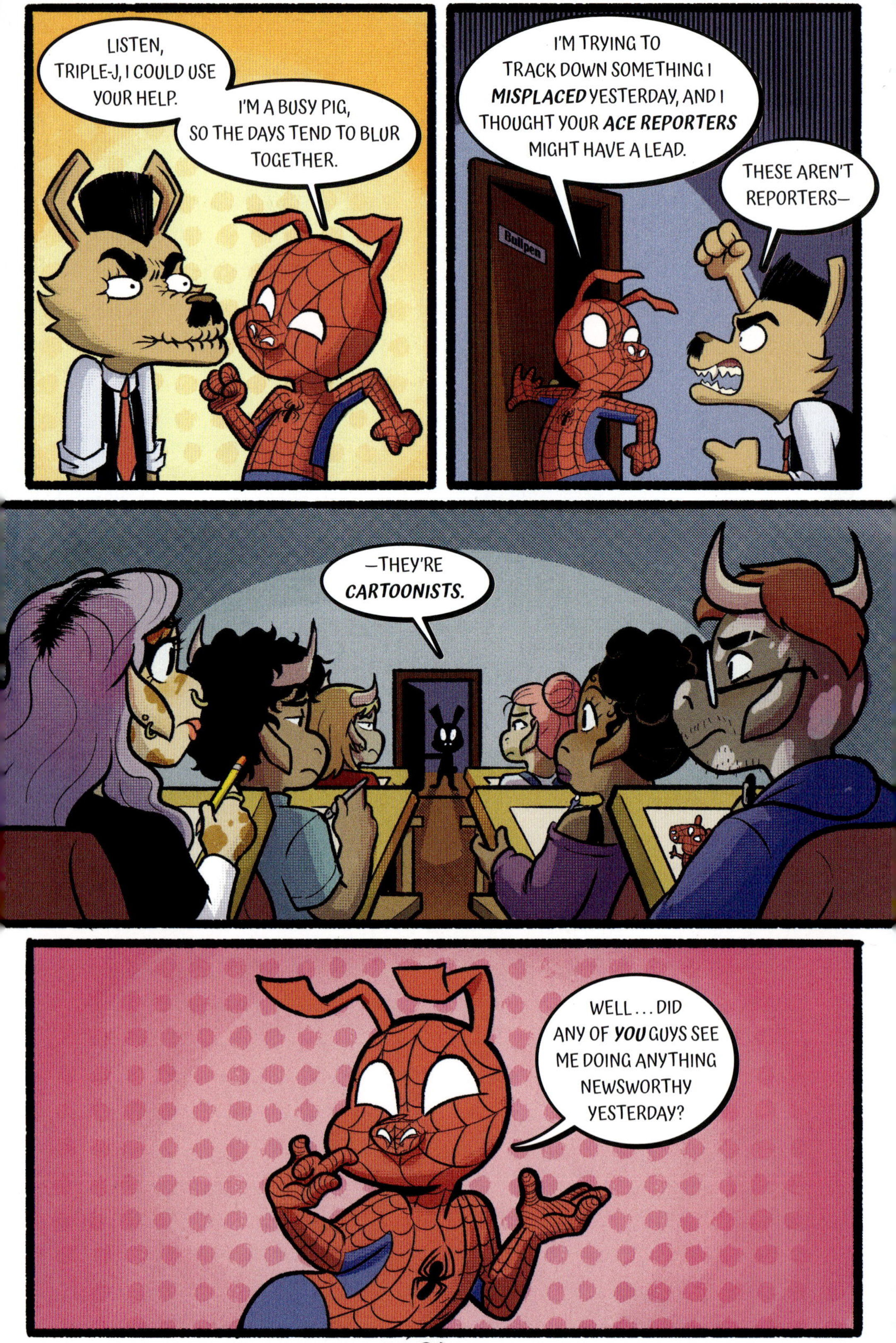
LISTEN, TRIPLE-J, I COULD USE YOUR HELP.
I'M A BUSY PIG, SO THE DAYS TEND TO BLUR TOGETHER.
I'M TRYING TO TRACK DOWN SOMETHING I MISPLACED YESTERDAY, AND I THOUGHT YOUR ACE REPORTERS MIGHT HAVE A LEAD.
Bullpen
THESE AREN'T REPORTERS—
—THEY'RE CARTOONISTS.
WELL . . . DID ANY OF YOU GUYS SEE ME DOING ANYTHING NEWSWORTHY YESTERDAY?

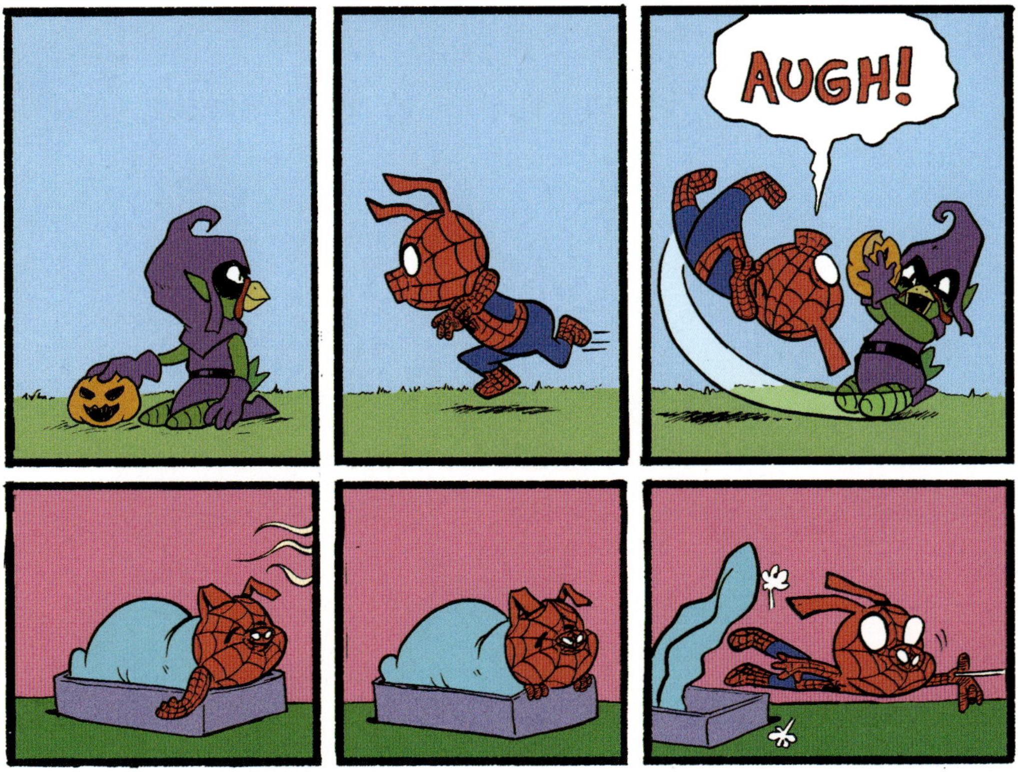
AUGH!

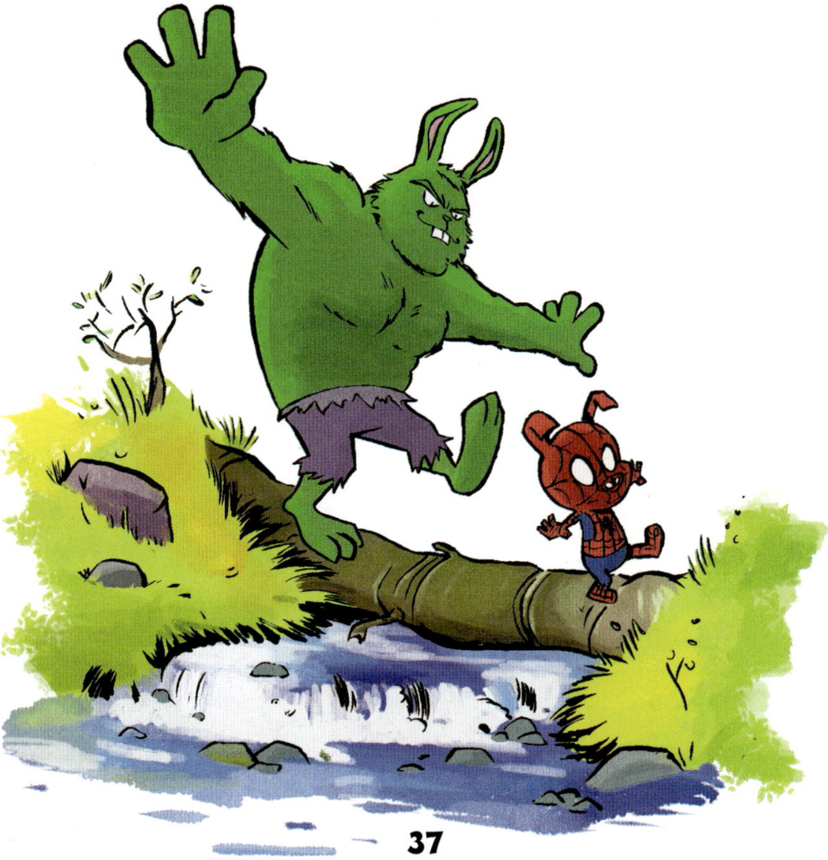

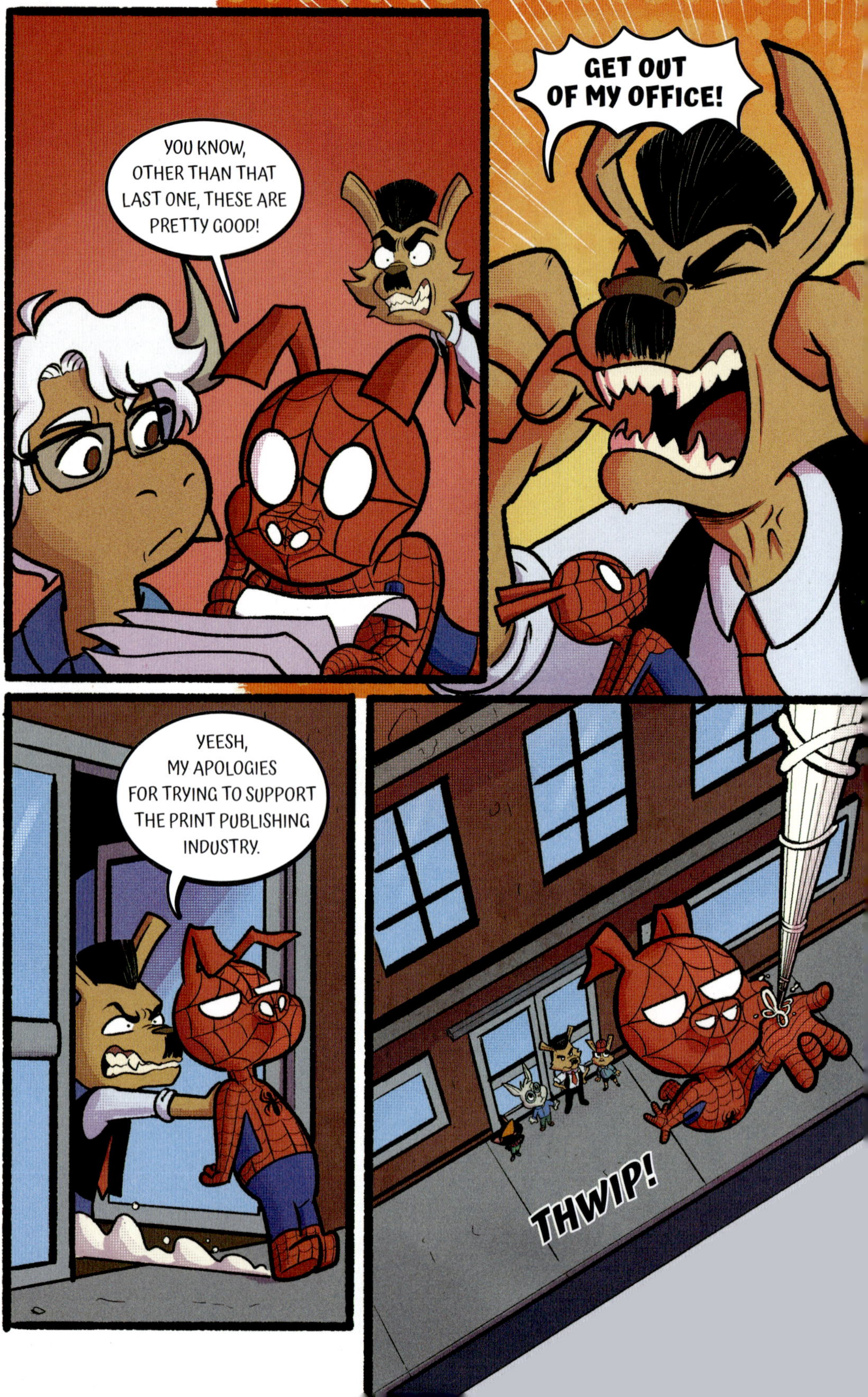
YOU KNOW, OTHER THAN THAT LAST ONE, THESE ARE PRETTY GOOD!
GET OUT OF MY OFFICE!
YEESH, MY APOLOGIES FOR TRYING TO SUPPORT THE PRINT PUBLISHING INDUSTRY.
THWIP!

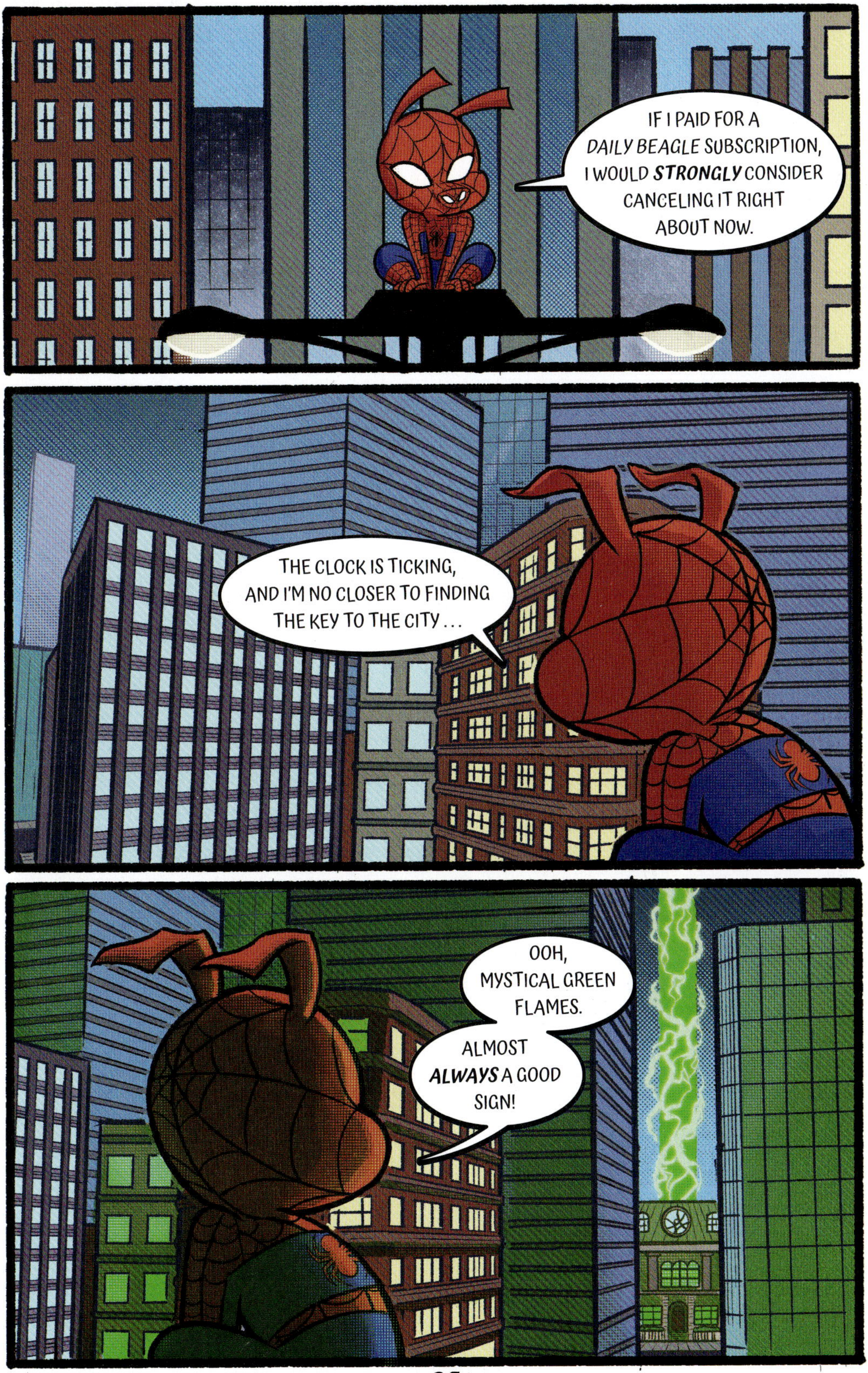
IF I PAID FOR A DAILY BEAGLE SUBSCRIPTION, I WOULD STRONGLY CONSIDER CANCELING IT RIGHT ABOUT NOW.
THE CLOCK IS TICKING, AND I'M NO CLOSER TO FINDING THE KEY TO THE CITY . . .
OOH, MYSTICAL GREEN FLAMES.
ALMOST ALWAYS A GOOD SIGN!

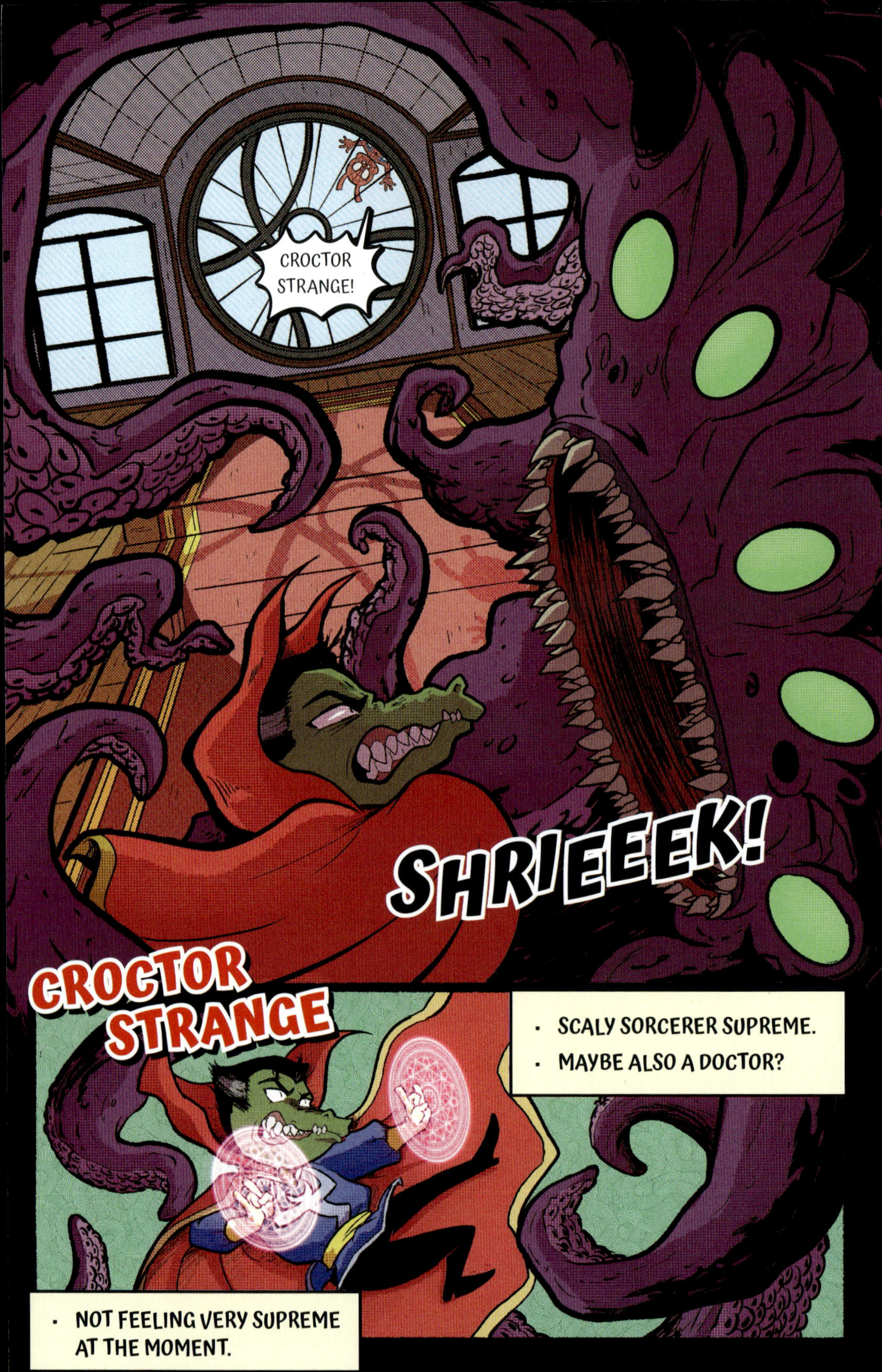
CROCTOR STRANGE!
SHRIEEEK!
CROCTOR STRANGE
· SCALY SORCERER SUPREME.
· MAYBE ALSO A DOCTOR?
· NOT FEELING VERY SUPREME AT THE MOMENT.

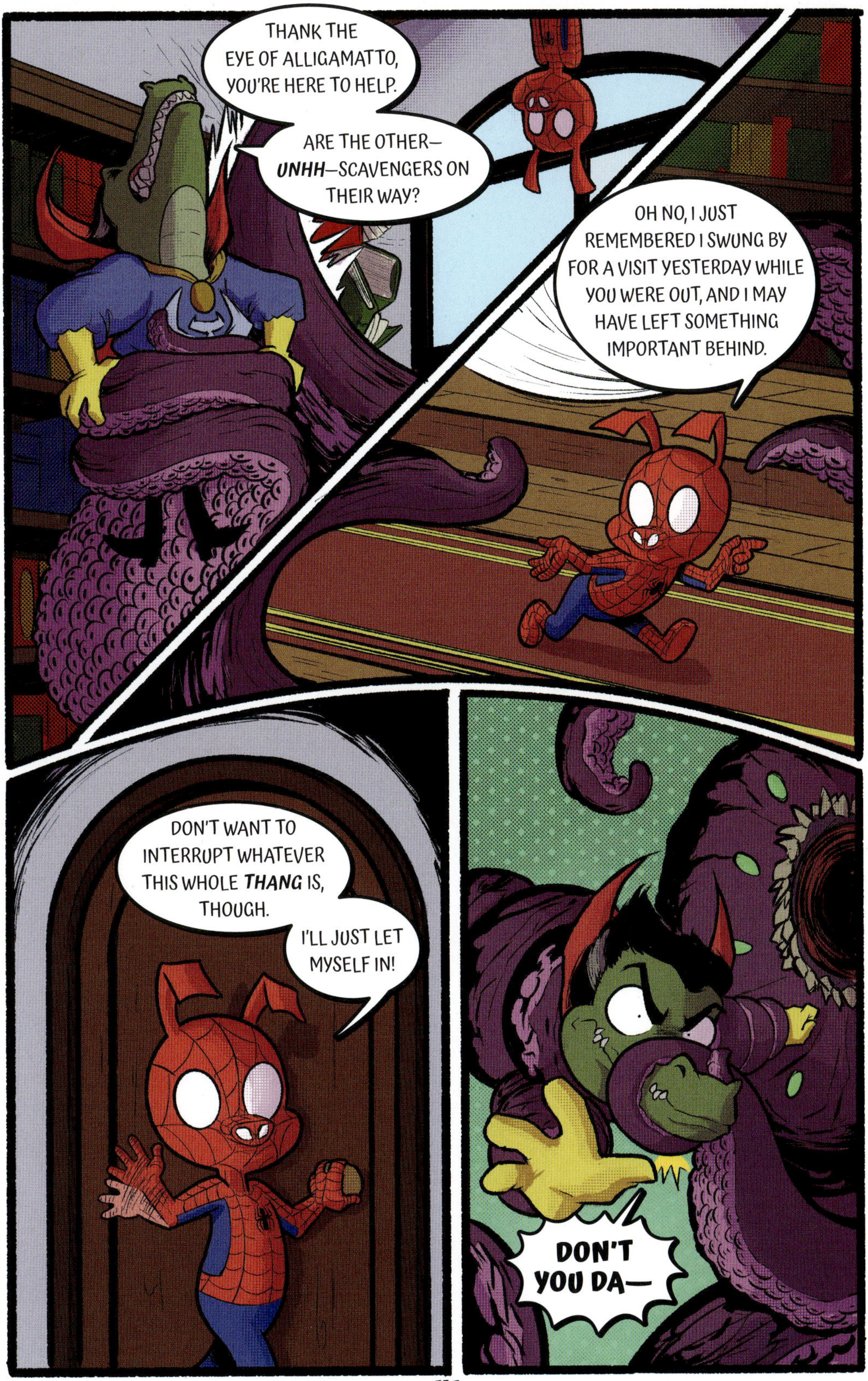
THANK THE EYE OF ALLIGAMATTO, YOU'RE HERE TO HELP.
ARE THE OTHER—*UNHH*—SCAVENGERS ON THEIR WAY?
OH NO, I JUST REMEMBERED I SWUNG BY FOR A VISIT YESTERDAY WHILE YOU WERE OUT, AND I MAY HAVE LEFT SOMETHING IMPORTANT BEHIND.
DON'T WANT TO INTERRUPT WHATEVER THIS WHOLE *THANG* IS, THOUGH.
I'LL JUST LET MYSELF IN!
DON'T YOU DA—

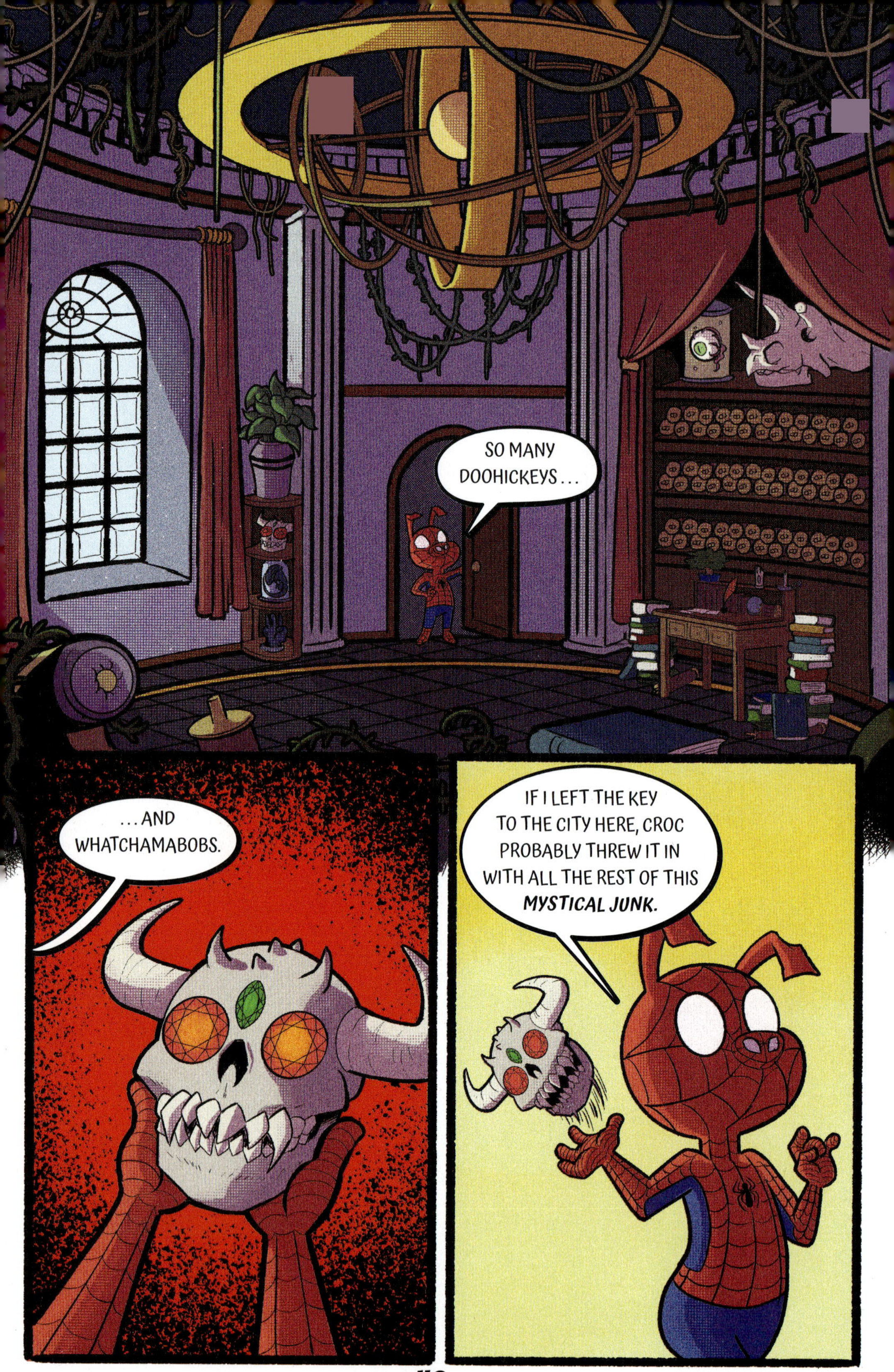
SO MANY DOOHICKEYS . . .
. . . AND WHATCHAMABOBS.
IF I LEFT THE KEY TO THE CITY HERE, CROC PROBABLY THREW IT IN WITH ALL THE REST OF THIS ***MYSTICAL JUNK.***

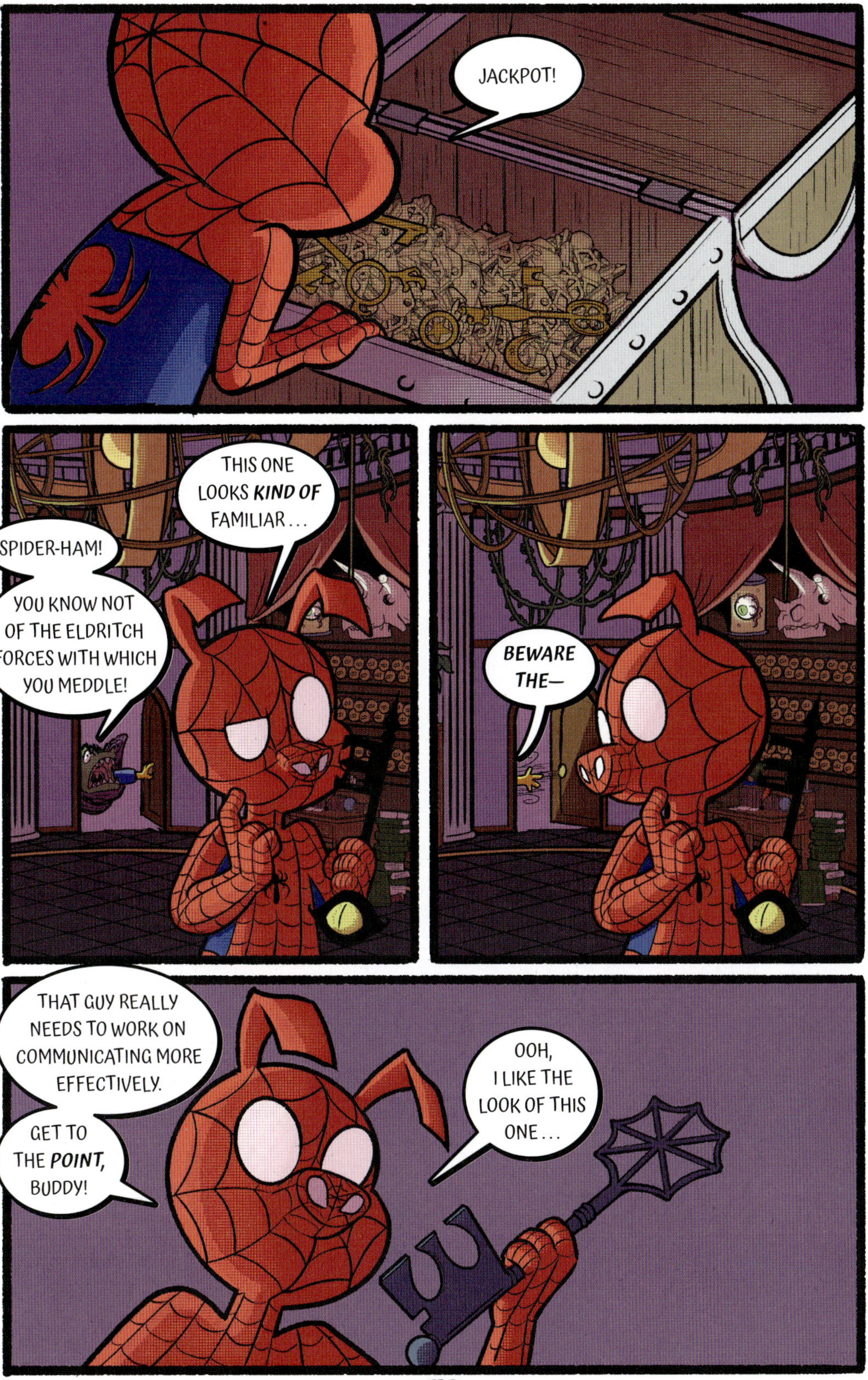
JACKPOT!
SPIDER-HAM!
YOU KNOW NOT OF THE ELDRITCH FORCES WITH WHICH YOU MEDDLE!
THIS ONE LOOKS **KIND OF** FAMILIAR . . .
BEWARE THE—
THAT GUY REALLY NEEDS TO WORK ON COMMUNICATING MORE EFFECTIVELY.
GET TO THE **POINT,** BUDDY!
OOH, I LIKE THE LOOK OF THIS ONE . . .

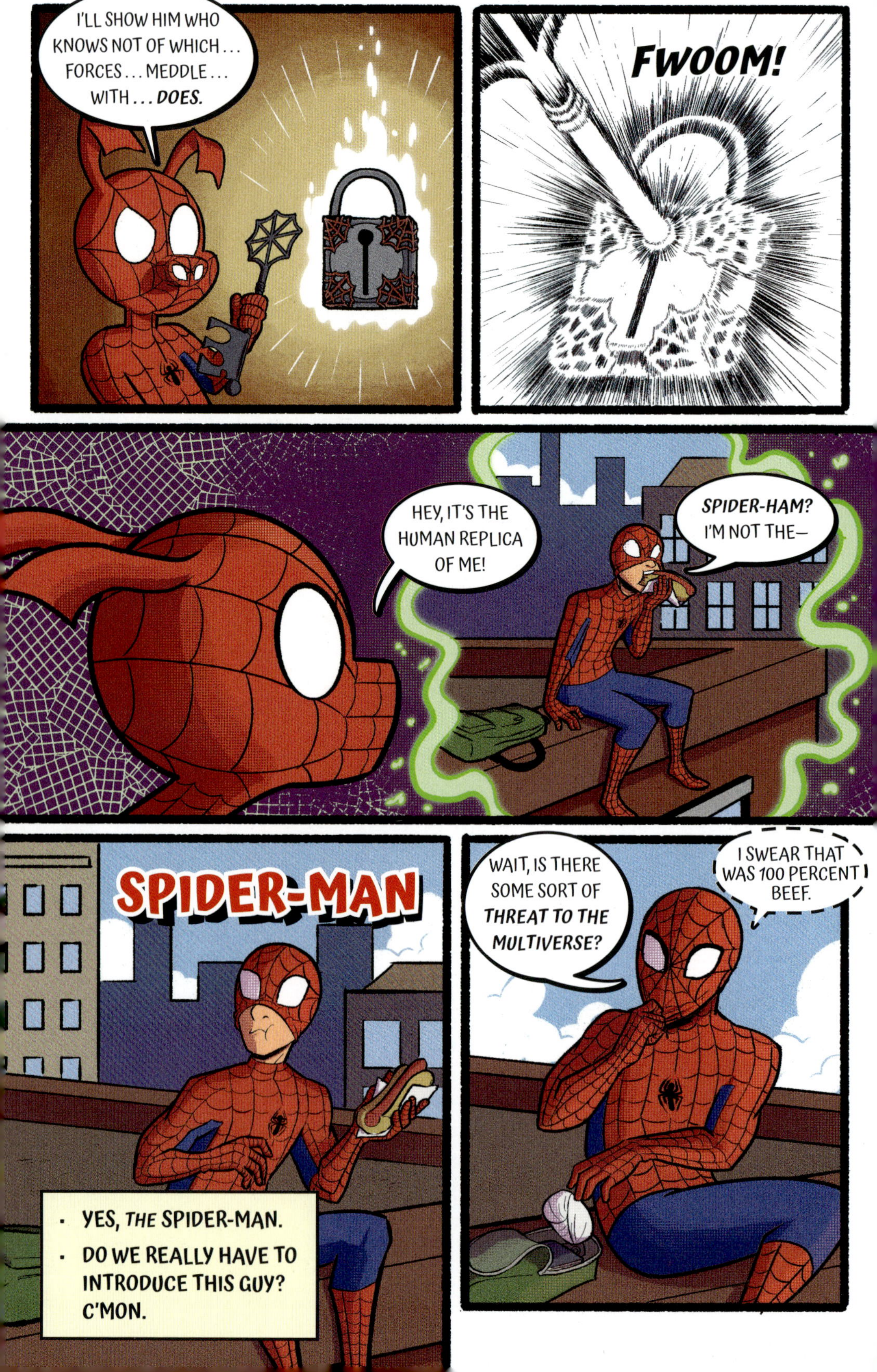
I'LL SHOW HIM WHO KNOWS NOT OF WHICH . . . FORCES . . . MEDDLE . . . WITH . . . DOES.
FWOOM!
HEY, IT'S THE HUMAN REPLICA OF ME!
SPIDER-HAM? I'M NOT THE—
SPIDER-MAN
YES, THE SPIDER-MAN.
DO WE REALLY HAVE TO INTRODUCE THIS GUY? C'MON.
WAIT, IS THERE SOME SORT OF THREAT TO THE MULTIVERSE?
I SWEAR THAT WAS 100 PERCENT BEEF.

MORE LIKE AN... *INCONVENIENCE* THAN A THREAT.

ONE THAT'S ALL MY FAULT. I THINK I REALLY LET NEW YOLK CITY DOWN THIS TIME.

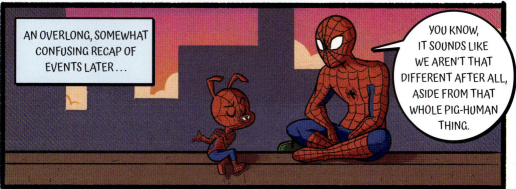

AN OVERLONG, SOMEWHAT CONFUSING RECAP OF EVENTS LATER...

YOU KNOW, IT SOUNDS LIKE WE AREN'T THAT DIFFERENT AFTER ALL, ASIDE FROM THAT WHOLE PIG-HUMAN THING.

TECHNICALLY, I'M A SPIDER WHO WAS BITTEN BY A RADIOACTIVE PIG—

YEAH, NO, I DON'T HAVE TIME FOR THAT NONSENSE TODAY.

EVEN THOUGH I'VE SAVED THE WORLD COUNTLESS TIMES, A LOT OF MY FELLOW HEROES STILL UNDERESTIMATE ME.

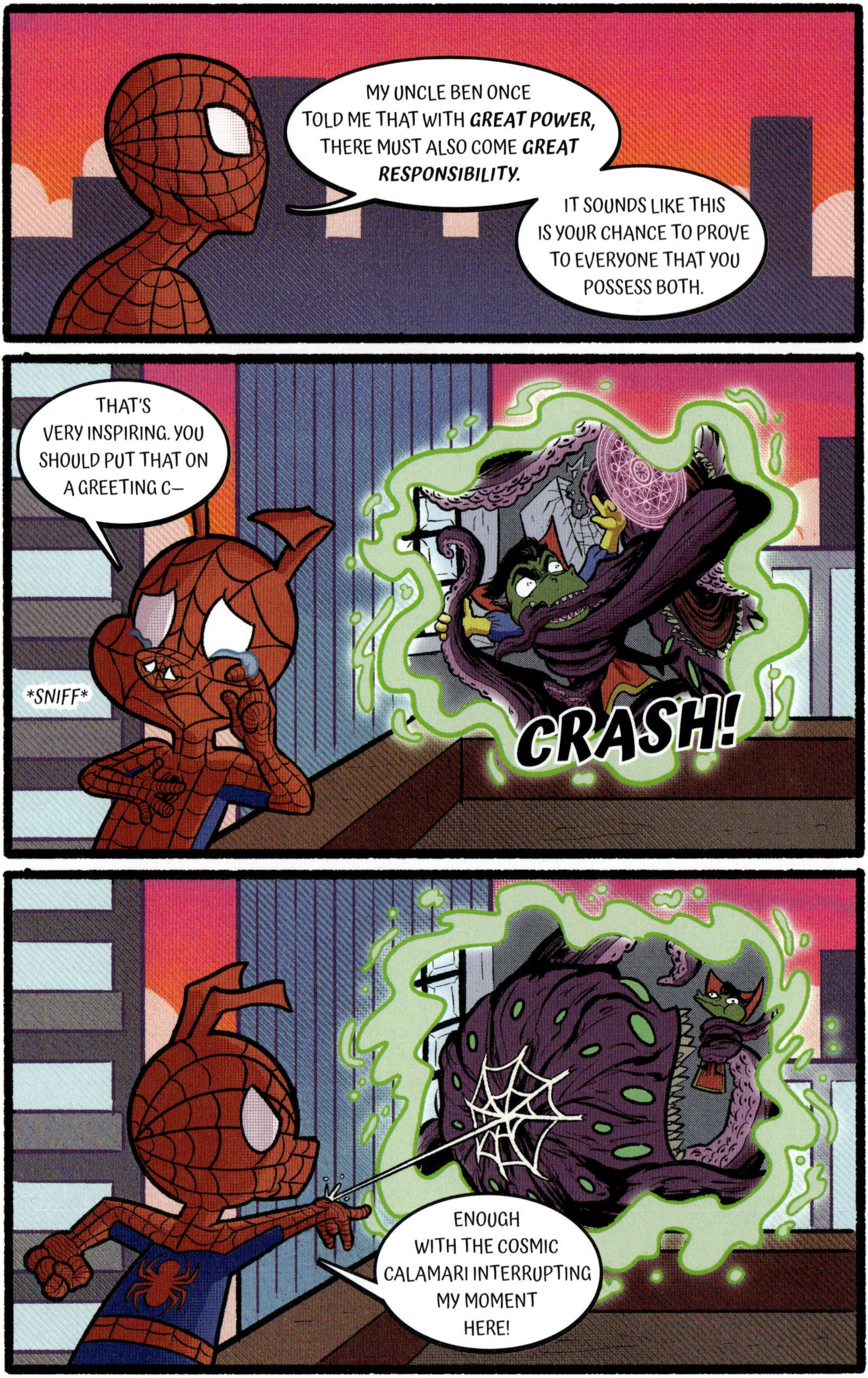
MY UNCLE BEN ONCE TOLD ME THAT WITH **GREAT POWER,** THERE MUST ALSO COME **GREAT RESPONSIBILITY.**
IT SOUNDS LIKE THIS IS YOUR CHANCE TO PROVE TO EVERYONE THAT YOU POSSESS BOTH.
THAT'S VERY INSPIRING. YOU SHOULD PUT THAT ON A GREETING C—
SNIFF
CRASH!
ENOUGH WITH THE COSMIC CALAMARI INTERRUPTING MY MOMENT HERE!

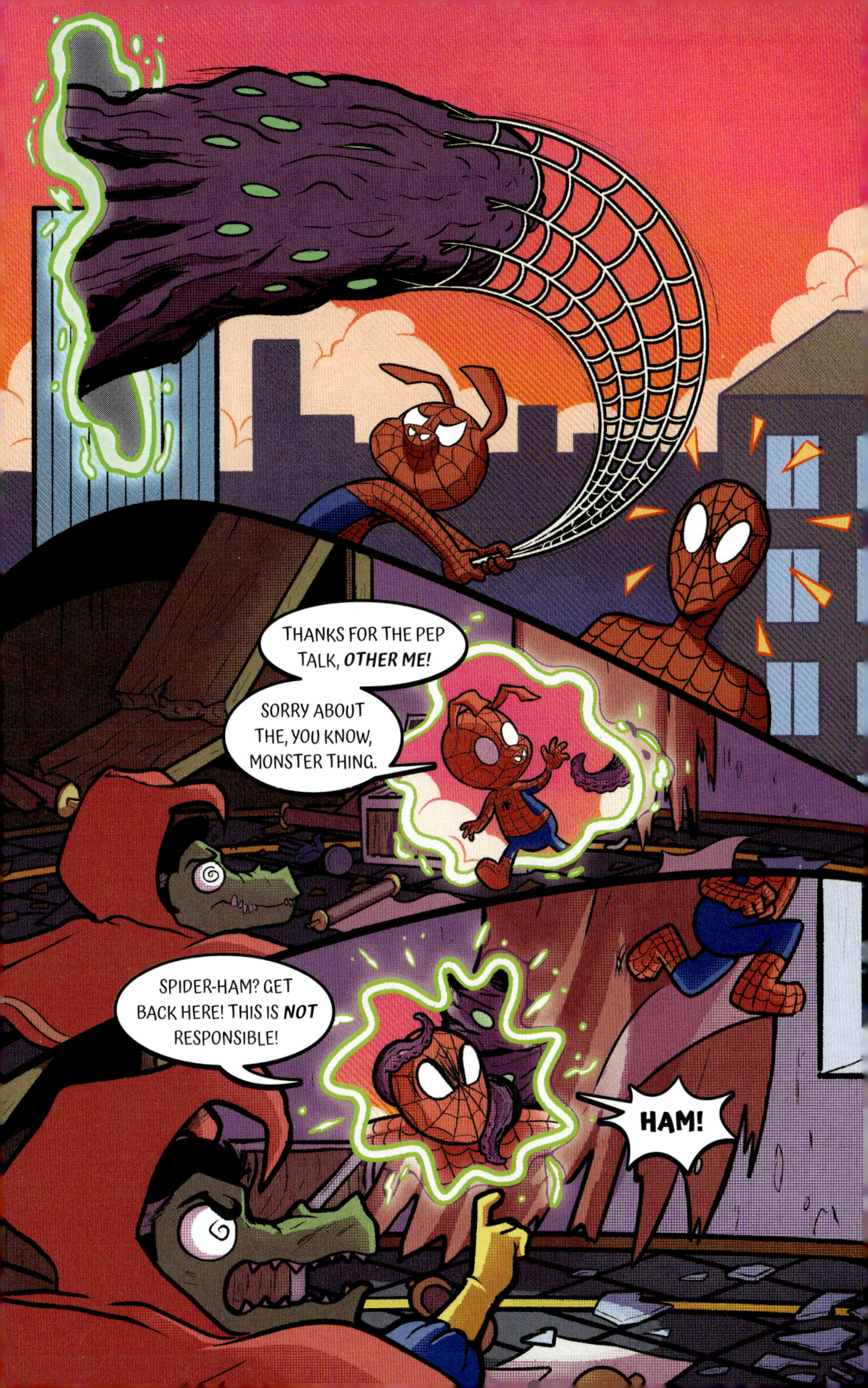
THANKS FOR THE PEP TALK, ***OTHER ME!***
SORRY ABOUT THE, YOU KNOW, MONSTER THING.
SPIDER-HAM? GET BACK HERE! THIS IS ***NOT*** RESPONSIBLE!
HAM!

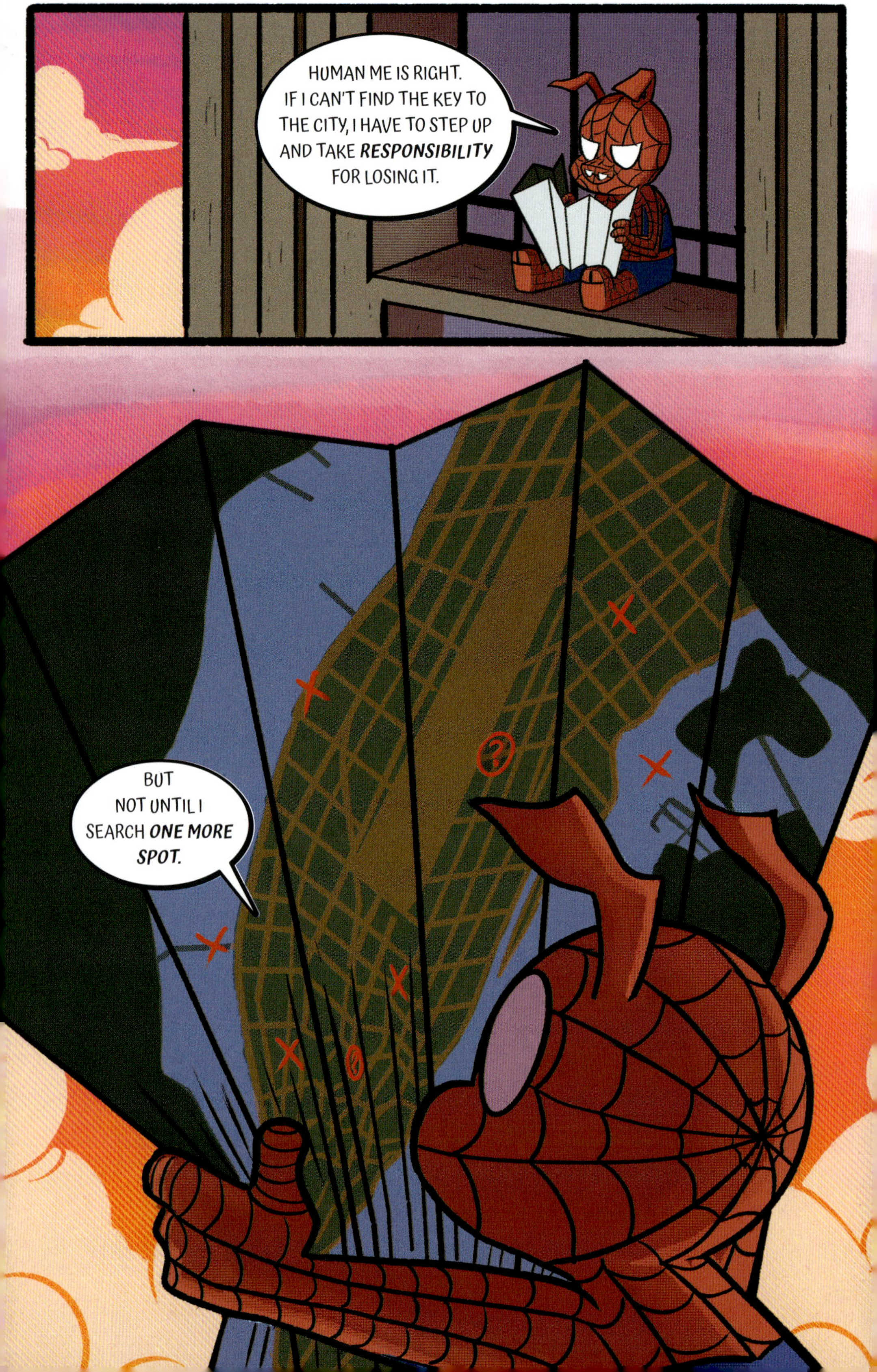
HUMAN ME IS RIGHT. IF I CAN'T FIND THE KEY TO THE CITY, I HAVE TO STEP UP AND TAKE **RESPONSIBILITY** FOR LOSING IT.
BUT NOT UNTIL I SEARCH **ONE MORE SPOT.**

CHAPTER TWO:

THE PIG
FINALE

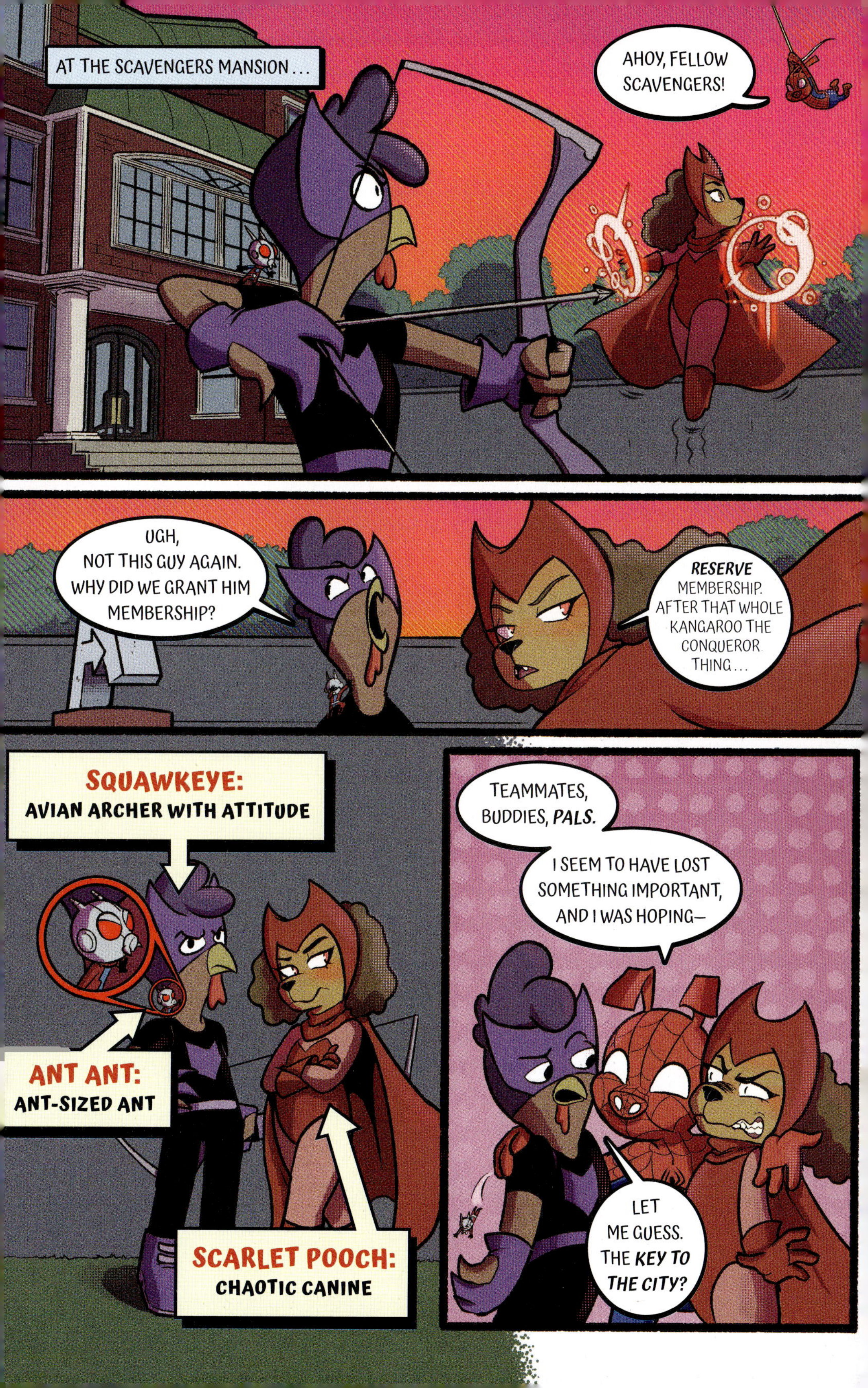

AT THE SCAVENGERS MANSION . . .
AHOY, FELLOW SCAVENGERS!
UGH, NOT THIS GUY AGAIN. WHY DID WE GRANT HIM MEMBERSHIP?
RESERVE MEMBERSHIP. AFTER THAT WHOLE KANGAROO THE CONQUEROR THING . . .
SQUAWKEYE: AVIAN ARCHER WITH ATTITUDE
ANT ANT: ANT-SIZED ANT
SCARLET POOCH: CHAOTIC CANINE
TEAMMATES, BUDDIES, PALS.
I SEEM TO HAVE LOST SOMETHING IMPORTANT, AND I WAS HOPING—
LET ME GUESS. THE KEY TO THE CITY?

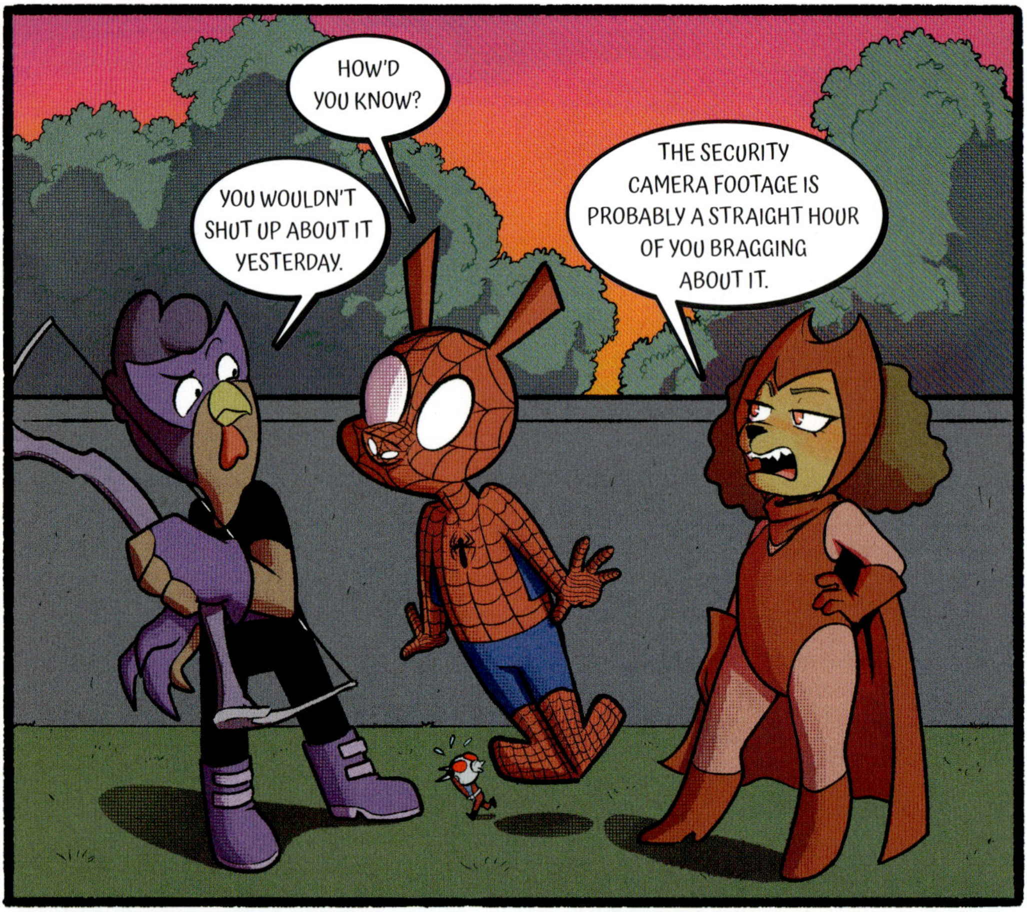
YOU WOULDN'T SHUT UP ABOUT IT YESTERDAY.
HOW'D YOU KNOW?
THE SECURITY CAMERA FOOTAGE IS PROBABLY A STRAIGHT HOUR OF YOU BRAGGING ABOUT IT.

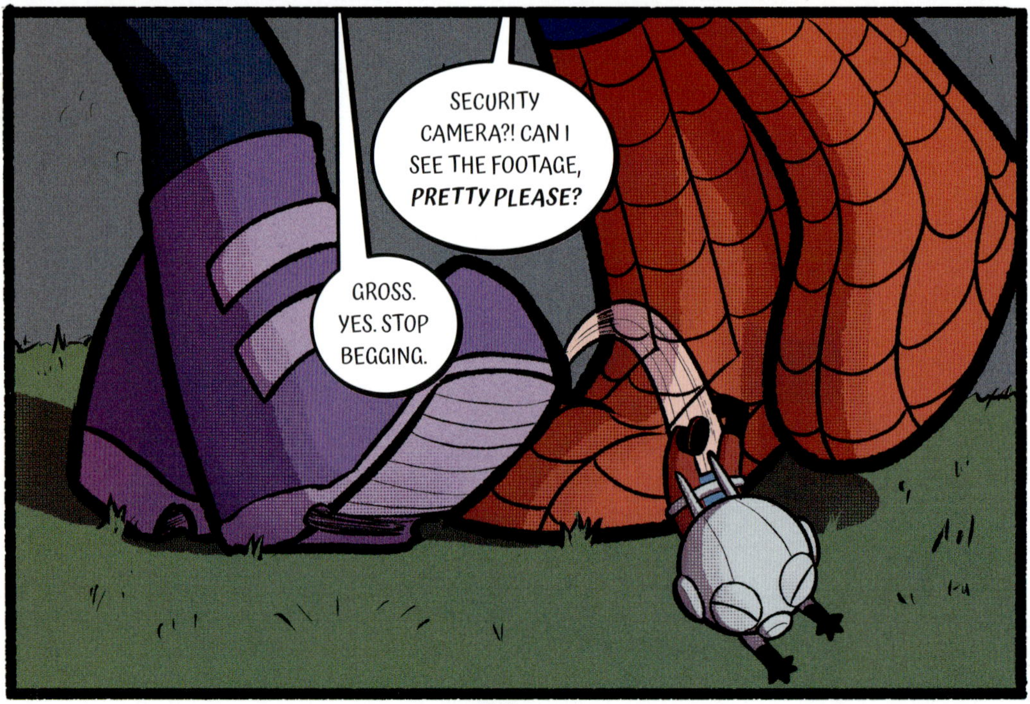
SECURITY CAMERA?! CAN I SEE THE FOOTAGE, ***PRETTY PLEASE?***
GROSS. YES. STOP BEGGING.

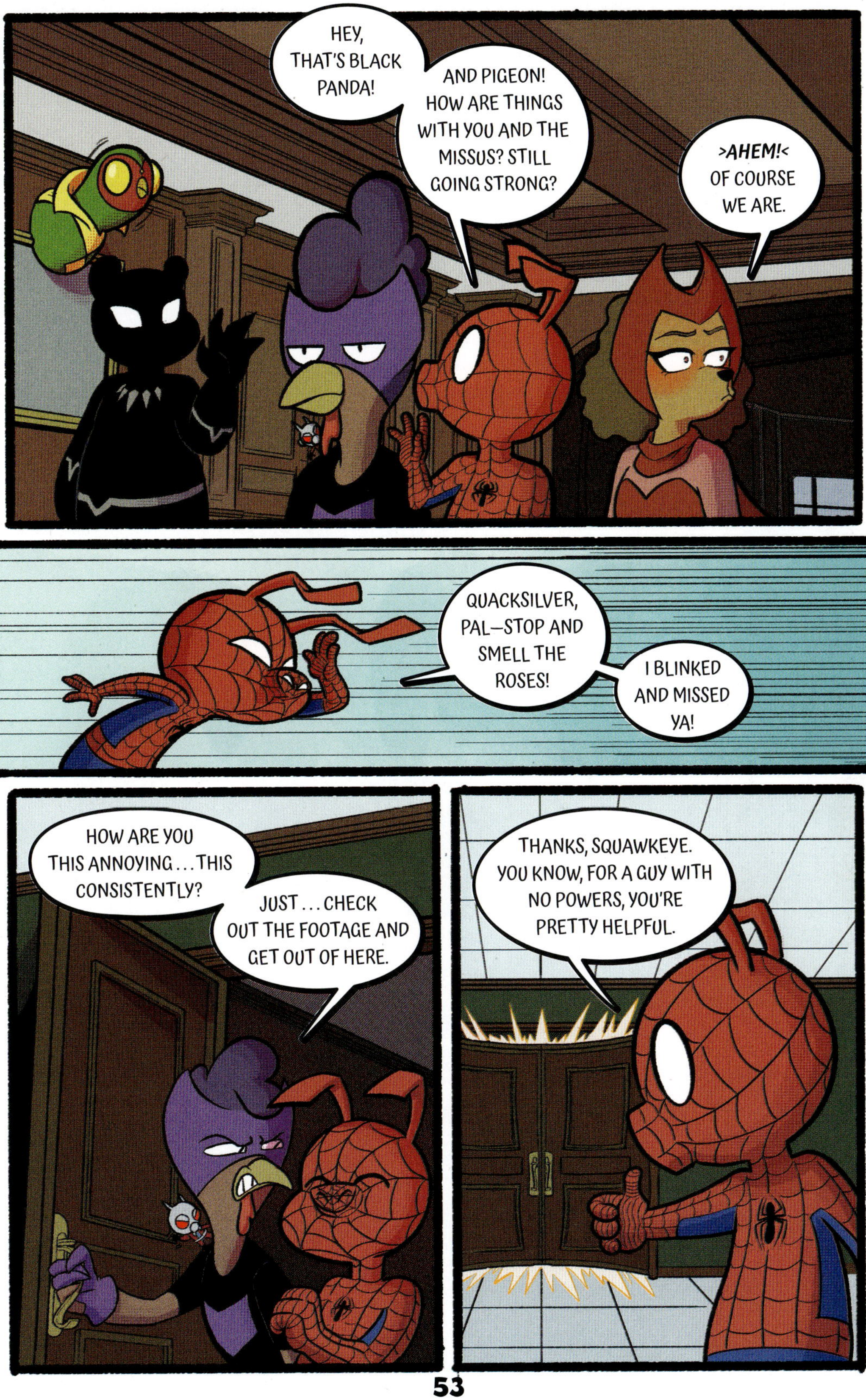
HEY, THAT'S BLACK PANDA!
AND PIGEON! HOW ARE THINGS WITH YOU AND THE MISSUS? STILL GOING STRONG?
>AHEM!< OF COURSE WE ARE.
QUACKSILVER, PAL—STOP AND SMELL THE ROSES!
I BLINKED AND MISSED YA!
HOW ARE YOU THIS ANNOYING . . . THIS CONSISTENTLY?
JUST . . . CHECK OUT THE FOOTAGE AND GET OUT OF HERE.
THANKS, SQUAWKEYE. YOU KNOW, FOR A GUY WITH NO POWERS, YOU'RE PRETTY HELPFUL.

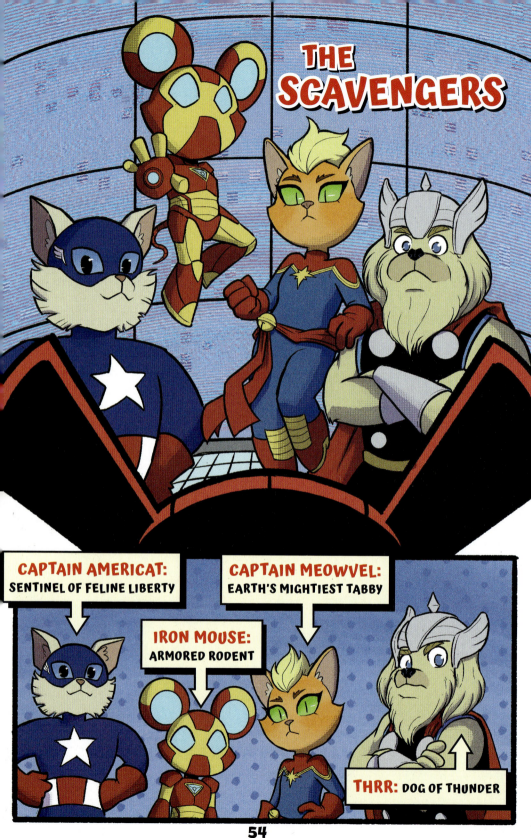

THE SCAVENGERS

CAPTAIN AMERICAT: SENTINEL OF FELINE LIBERTY

CAPTAIN MEOWVEL: EARTH'S MIGHTIEST TABBY

IRON MOUSE: ARMORED RODENT

THRR: DOG OF THUNDER

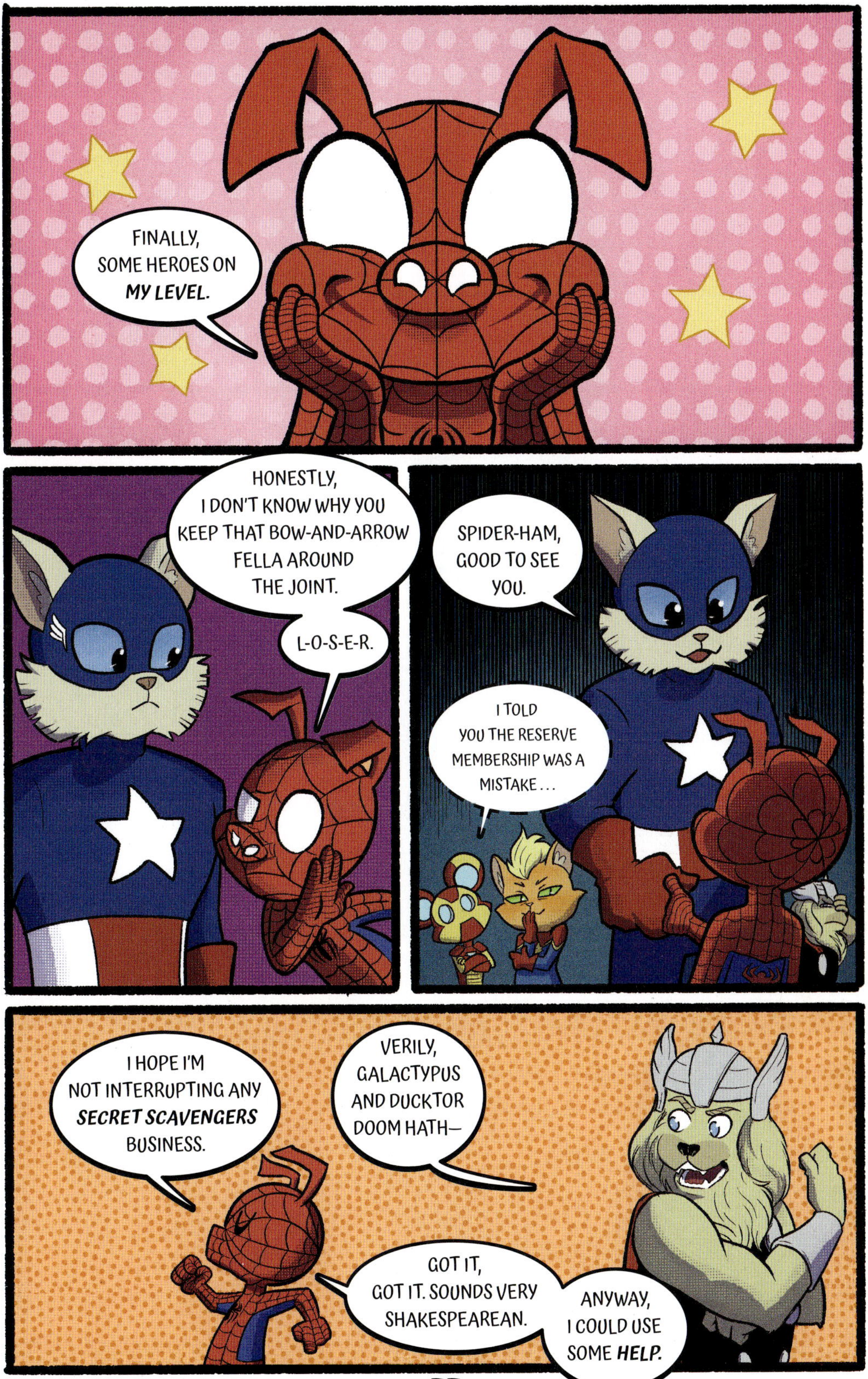
FINALLY, SOME HEROES ON **MY LEVEL.**
HONESTLY, I DON'T KNOW WHY YOU KEEP THAT BOW-AND-ARROW FELLA AROUND THE JOINT.
L-O-S-E-R.
SPIDER-HAM, GOOD TO SEE YOU.
I TOLD YOU THE RESERVE MEMBERSHIP WAS A MISTAKE...
I HOPE I'M NOT INTERRUPTING ANY ***SECRET SCAVENGERS*** BUSINESS.
VERILY, GALACTYPUS AND DUCKTOR DOOM HATH—
GOT IT, GOT IT. SOUNDS VERY SHAKESPEAREAN.
ANYWAY, I COULD USE SOME ***HELP.***

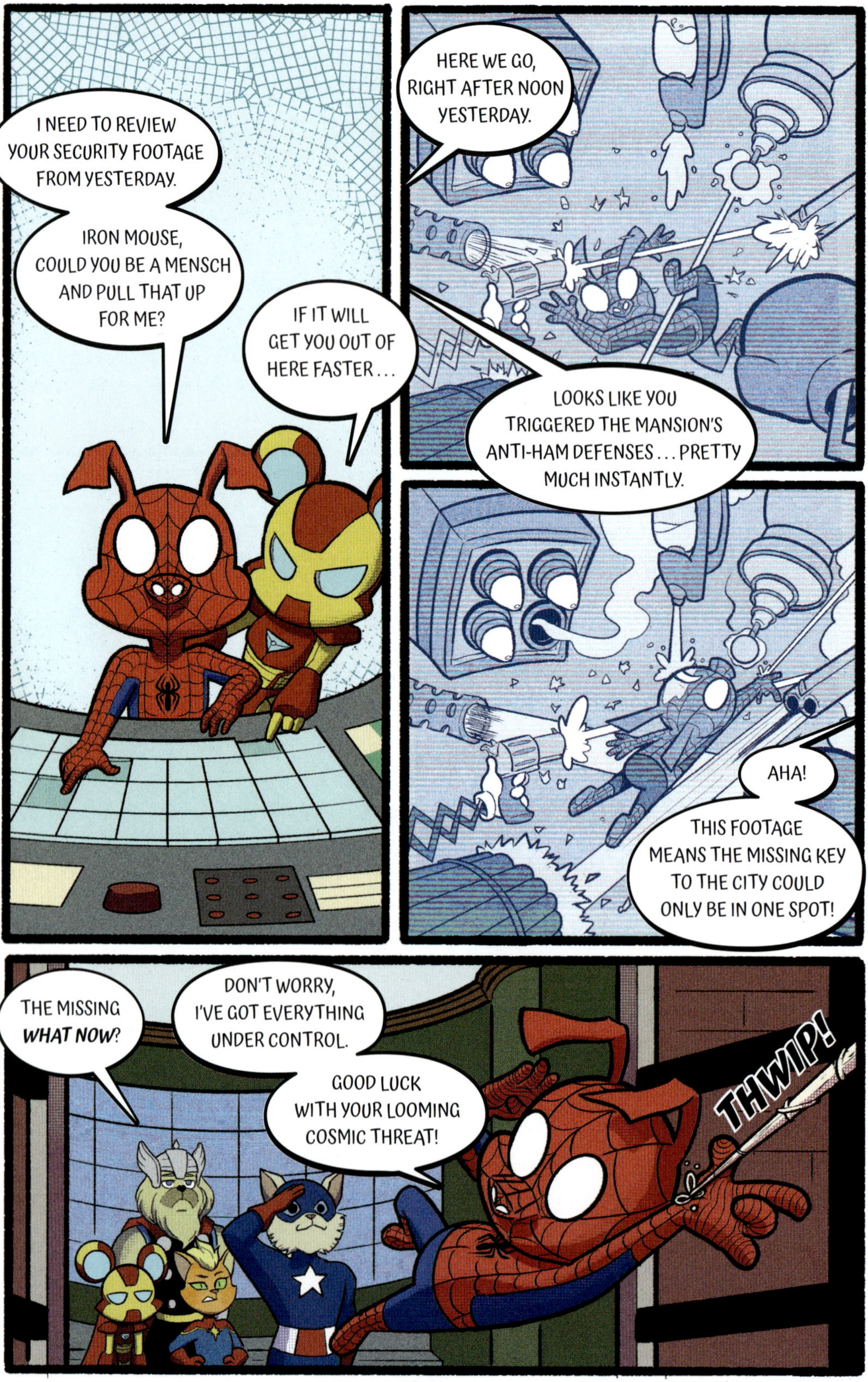
I NEED TO REVIEW YOUR SECURITY FOOTAGE FROM YESTERDAY.
IRON MOUSE, COULD YOU BE A MENSCH AND PULL THAT UP FOR ME?
IF IT WILL GET YOU OUT OF HERE FASTER . . .
HERE WE GO, RIGHT AFTER NOON YESTERDAY.
LOOKS LIKE YOU TRIGGERED THE MANSION'S ANTI-HAM DEFENSES . . . PRETTY MUCH INSTANTLY.
AHA!
THIS FOOTAGE MEANS THE MISSING KEY TO THE CITY COULD ONLY BE IN ONE SPOT!
THE MISSING *WHAT NOW*?
DON'T WORRY, I'VE GOT EVERYTHING UNDER CONTROL.
GOOD LUCK WITH YOUR LOOMING COSMIC THREAT!
THWIP!

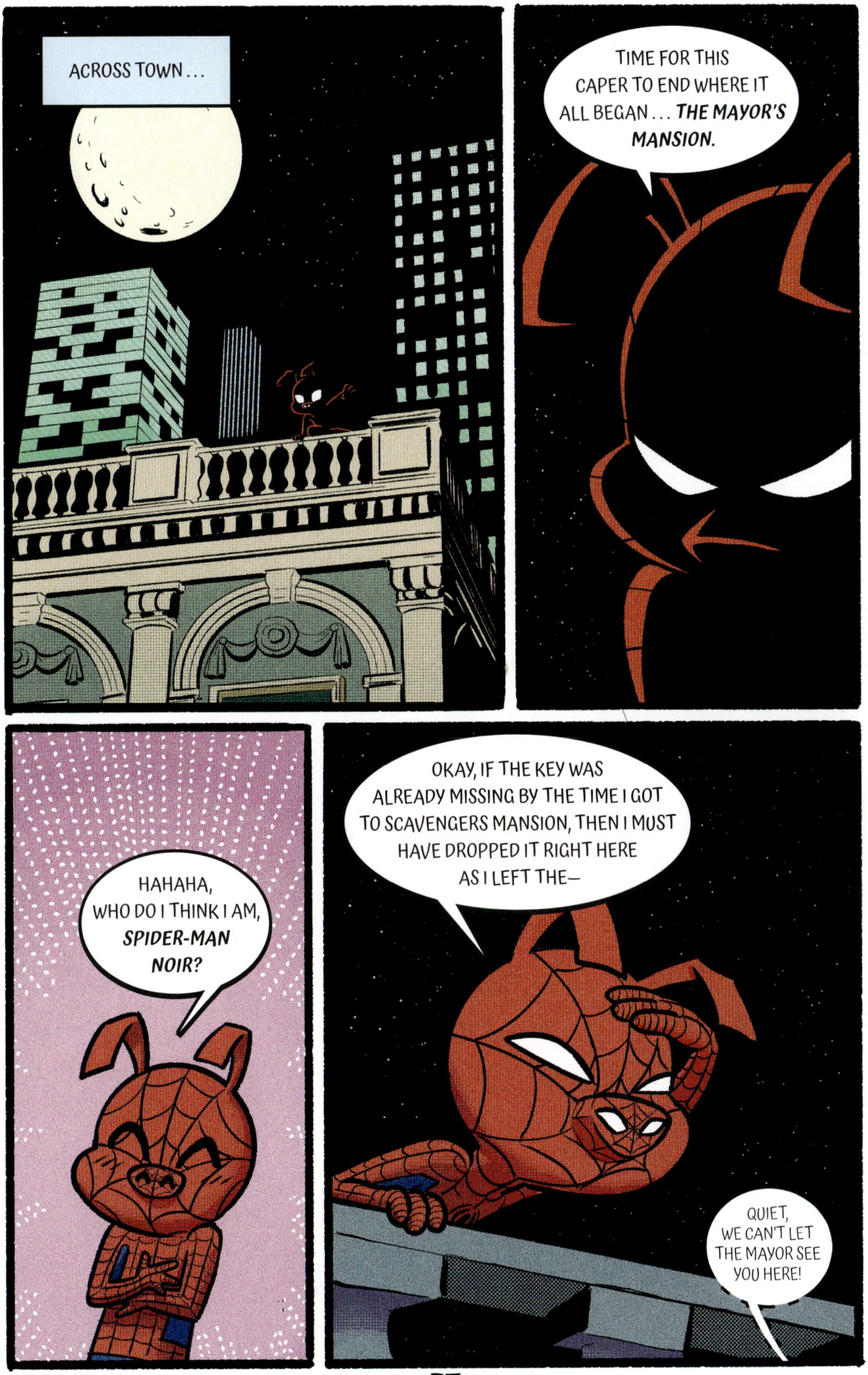
ACROSS TOWN . . .
TIME FOR THIS CAPER TO END WHERE IT ALL BEGAN . . . **THE MAYOR'S MANSION.**
HAHAHA, WHO DO I THINK I AM, **SPIDER-MAN NOIR?**
OKAY, IF THE KEY WAS ALREADY MISSING BY THE TIME I GOT TO SCAVENGERS MANSION, THEN I MUST HAVE DROPPED IT RIGHT HERE AS I LEFT THE—
QUIET, WE CAN'T LET THE MAYOR SEE YOU HERE!

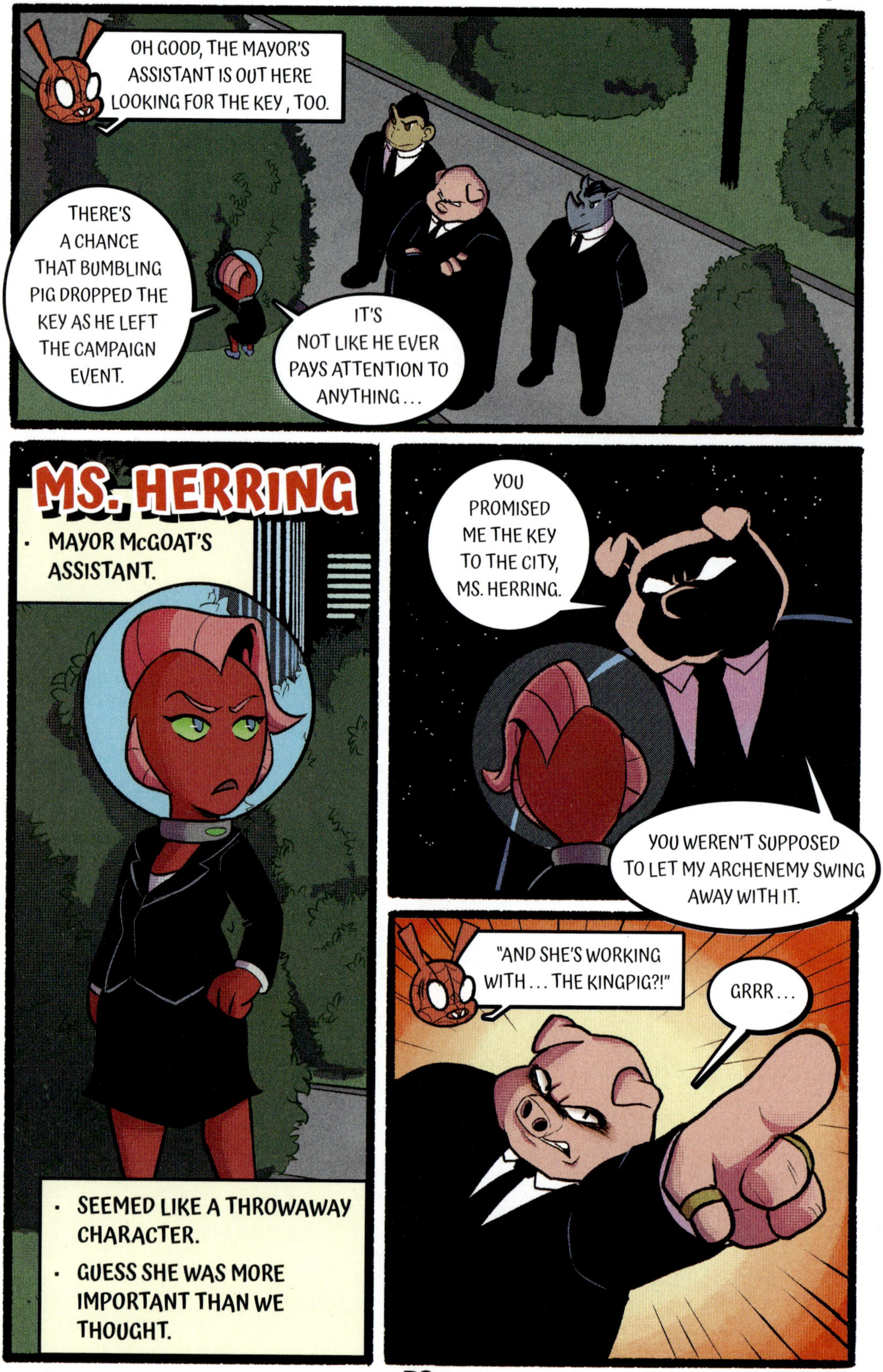
OH GOOD, THE MAYOR'S ASSISTANT IS OUT HERE LOOKING FOR THE KEY, TOO.
THERE'S A CHANCE THAT BUMBLING PIG DROPPED THE KEY AS HE LEFT THE CAMPAIGN EVENT.
IT'S NOT LIKE HE EVER PAYS ATTENTION TO ANYTHING...
MS. HERRING
• MAYOR McGOAT'S ASSISTANT.
• SEEMED LIKE A THROWAWAY CHARACTER.
• GUESS SHE WAS MORE IMPORTANT THAN WE THOUGHT.
YOU PROMISED ME THE KEY TO THE CITY, MS. HERRING.
YOU WEREN'T SUPPOSED TO LET MY ARCHENEMY SWING AWAY WITH IT.
"AND SHE'S WORKING WITH... THE KINGPIG?!"
GRRR...

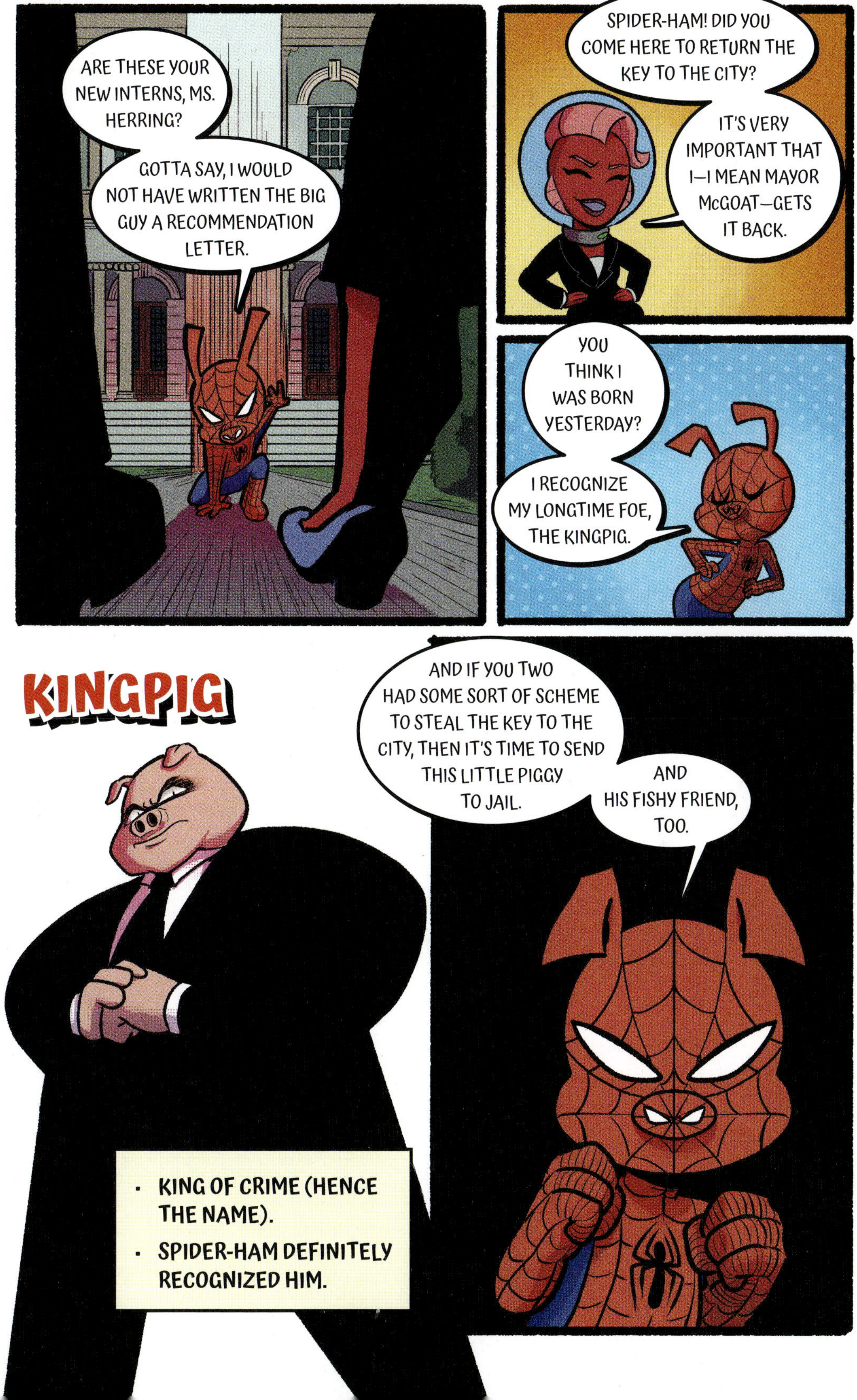
ARE THESE YOUR NEW INTERNS, MS. HERRING?
GOTTA SAY, I WOULD NOT HAVE WRITTEN THE BIG GUY A RECOMMENDATION LETTER.
SPIDER-HAM! DID YOU COME HERE TO RETURN THE KEY TO THE CITY?
IT'S VERY IMPORTANT THAT I—I MEAN MAYOR McGOAT—GETS IT BACK.
YOU THINK I WAS BORN YESTERDAY?
I RECOGNIZE MY LONGTIME FOE, THE KINGPIG.
KINGPIG
• KING OF CRIME (HENCE THE NAME).
• SPIDER-HAM DEFINITELY RECOGNIZED HIM.
AND IF YOU TWO HAD SOME SORT OF SCHEME TO STEAL THE KEY TO THE CITY, THEN IT'S TIME TO SEND THIS LITTLE PIGGY TO JAIL.
AND HIS FISHY FRIEND, TOO.

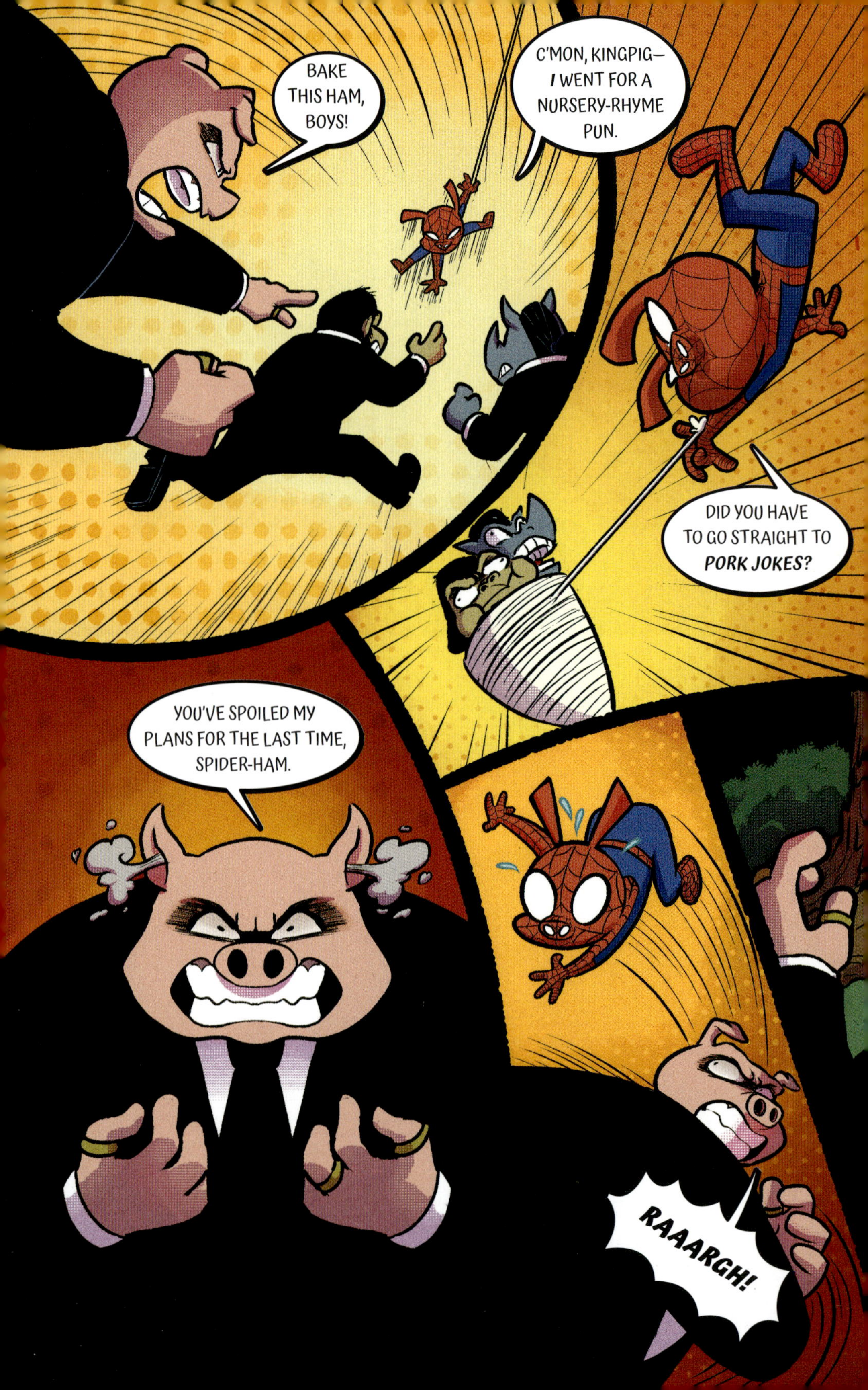
BAKE THIS HAM, BOYS!
C'MON, KINGPIG—I WENT FOR A NURSERY-RHYME PUN.
DID YOU HAVE TO GO STRAIGHT TO PORK JOKES?
YOU'VE SPOILED MY PLANS FOR THE LAST TIME, SPIDER-HAM.
RAAARGH!

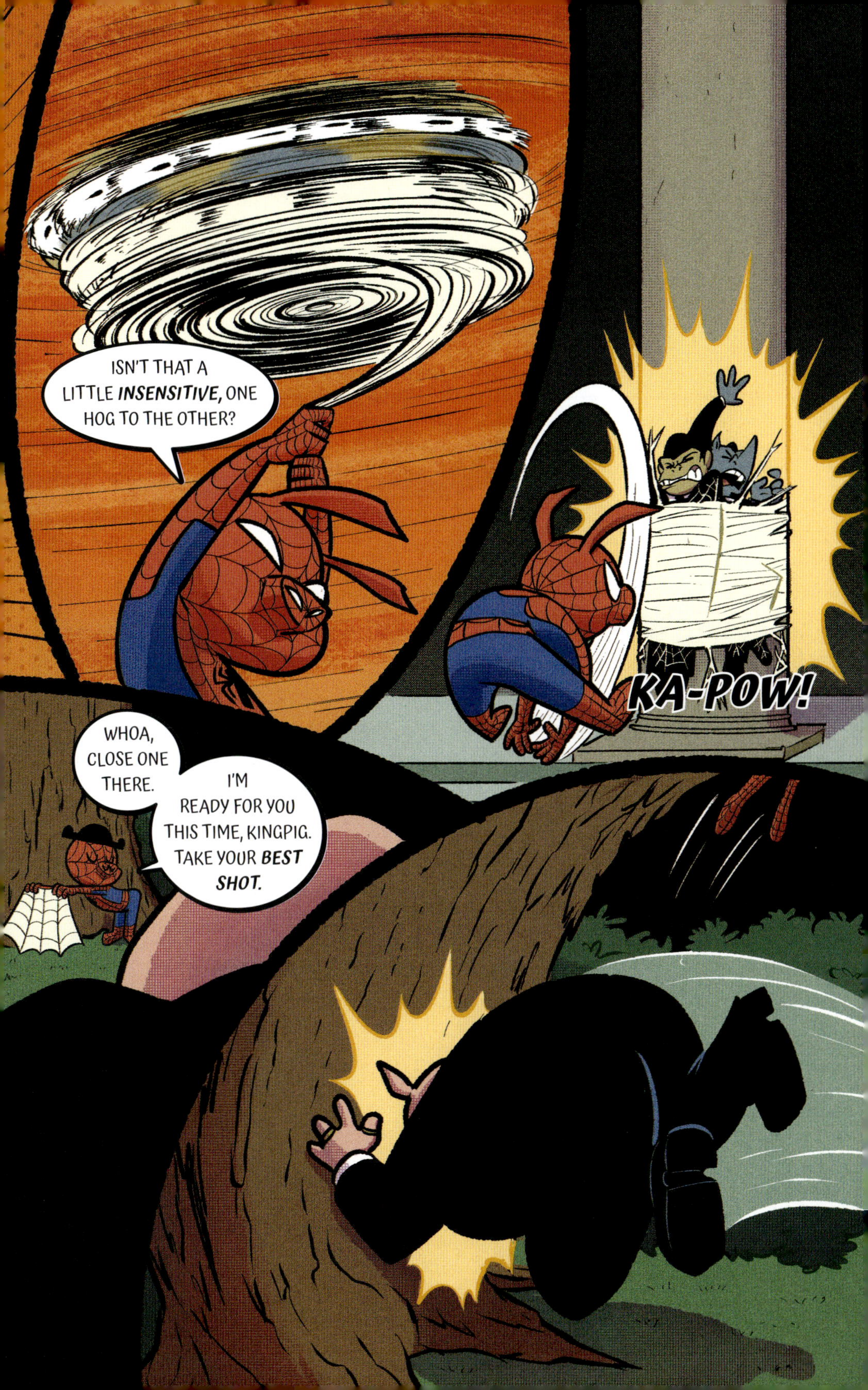
ISN'T THAT A LITTLE INSENSITIVE, ONE HOG TO THE OTHER?
KA-POW!
WHOA, CLOSE ONE THERE.
I'M READY FOR YOU THIS TIME, KINGPIG. TAKE YOUR BEST SHOT.

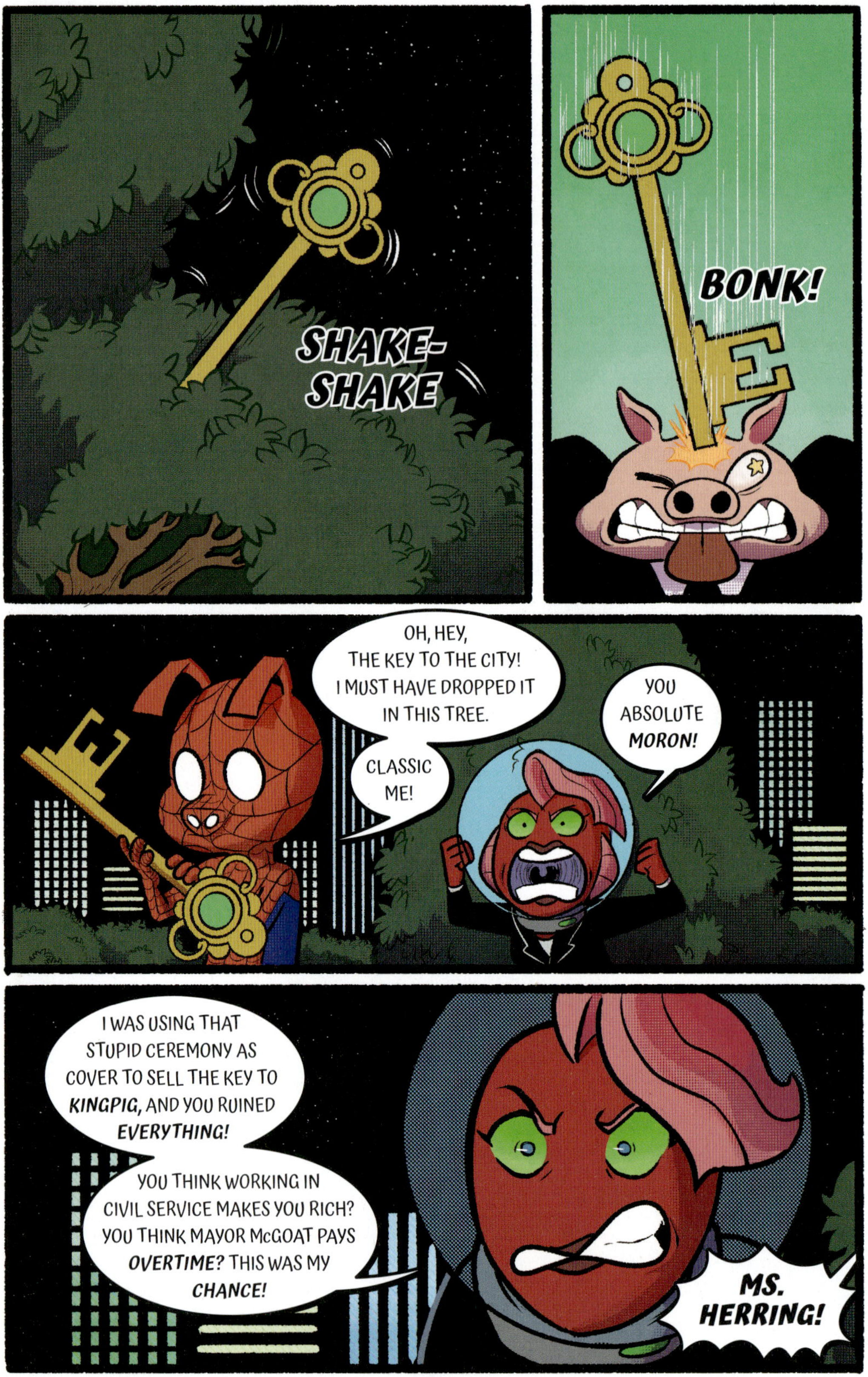
SHAKE-SHAKE
BONK!
OH, HEY, THE KEY TO THE CITY! I MUST HAVE DROPPED IT IN THIS TREE.
CLASSIC ME!
YOU ABSOLUTE MORON!
I WAS USING THAT STUPID CEREMONY AS COVER TO SELL THE KEY TO KINGPIG, AND YOU RUINED EVERYTHING!
YOU THINK WORKING IN CIVIL SERVICE MAKES YOU RICH? YOU THINK MAYOR McGOAT PAYS OVERTIME? THIS WAS MY CHANCE!
MS. HERRING!

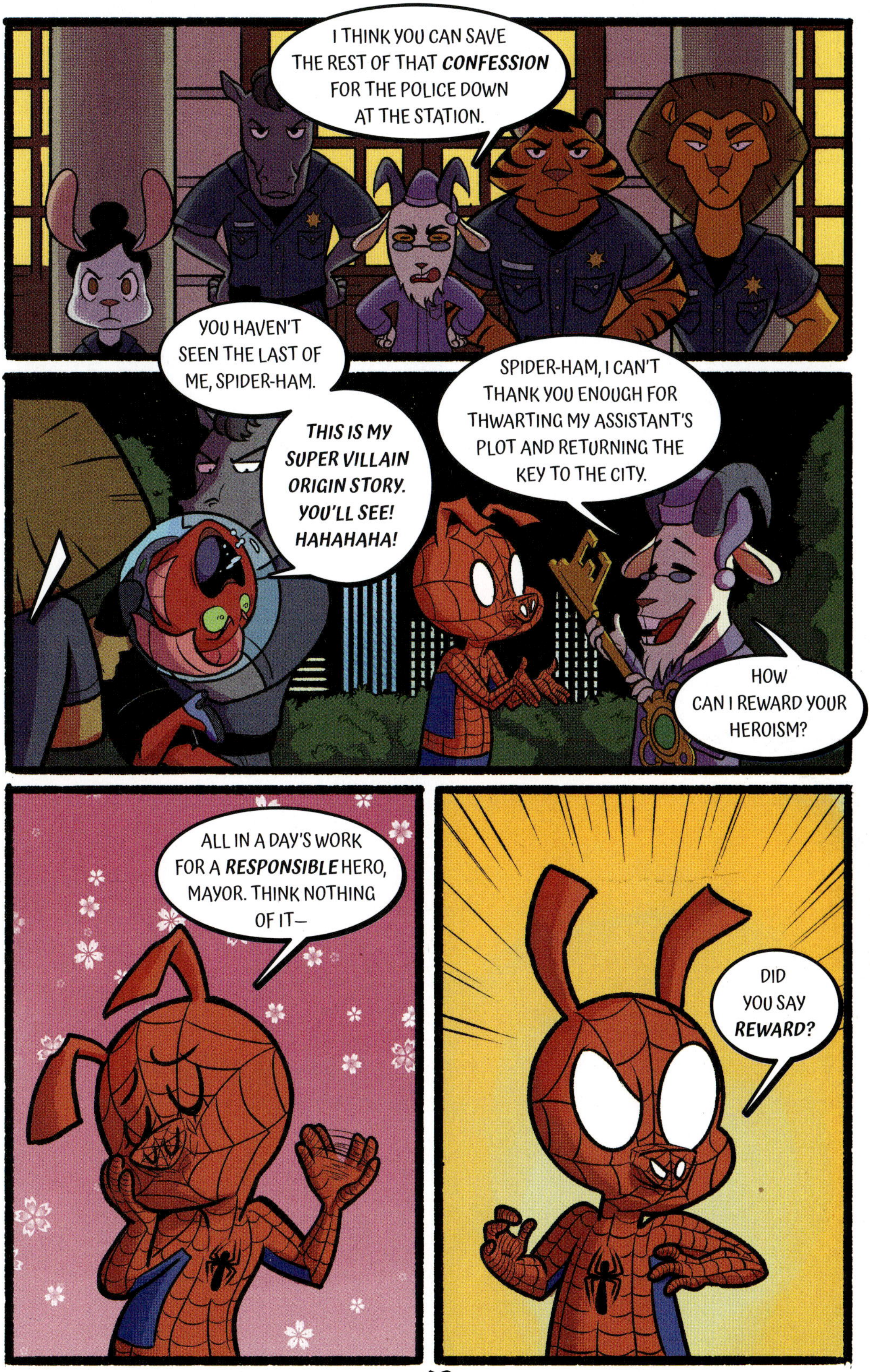
I THINK YOU CAN SAVE THE REST OF THAT **CONFESSION** FOR THE POLICE DOWN AT THE STATION.
YOU HAVEN'T SEEN THE LAST OF ME, SPIDER-HAM.
THIS IS MY SUPER VILLAIN ORIGIN STORY. YOU'LL SEE! HAHAHAHA!
SPIDER-HAM, I CAN'T THANK YOU ENOUGH FOR THWARTING MY ASSISTANT'S PLOT AND RETURNING THE KEY TO THE CITY.
HOW CAN I REWARD YOUR HEROISM?
ALL IN A DAY'S WORK FOR A **RESPONSIBLE** HERO, MAYOR. THINK NOTHING OF IT—
DID YOU SAY **REWARD?**

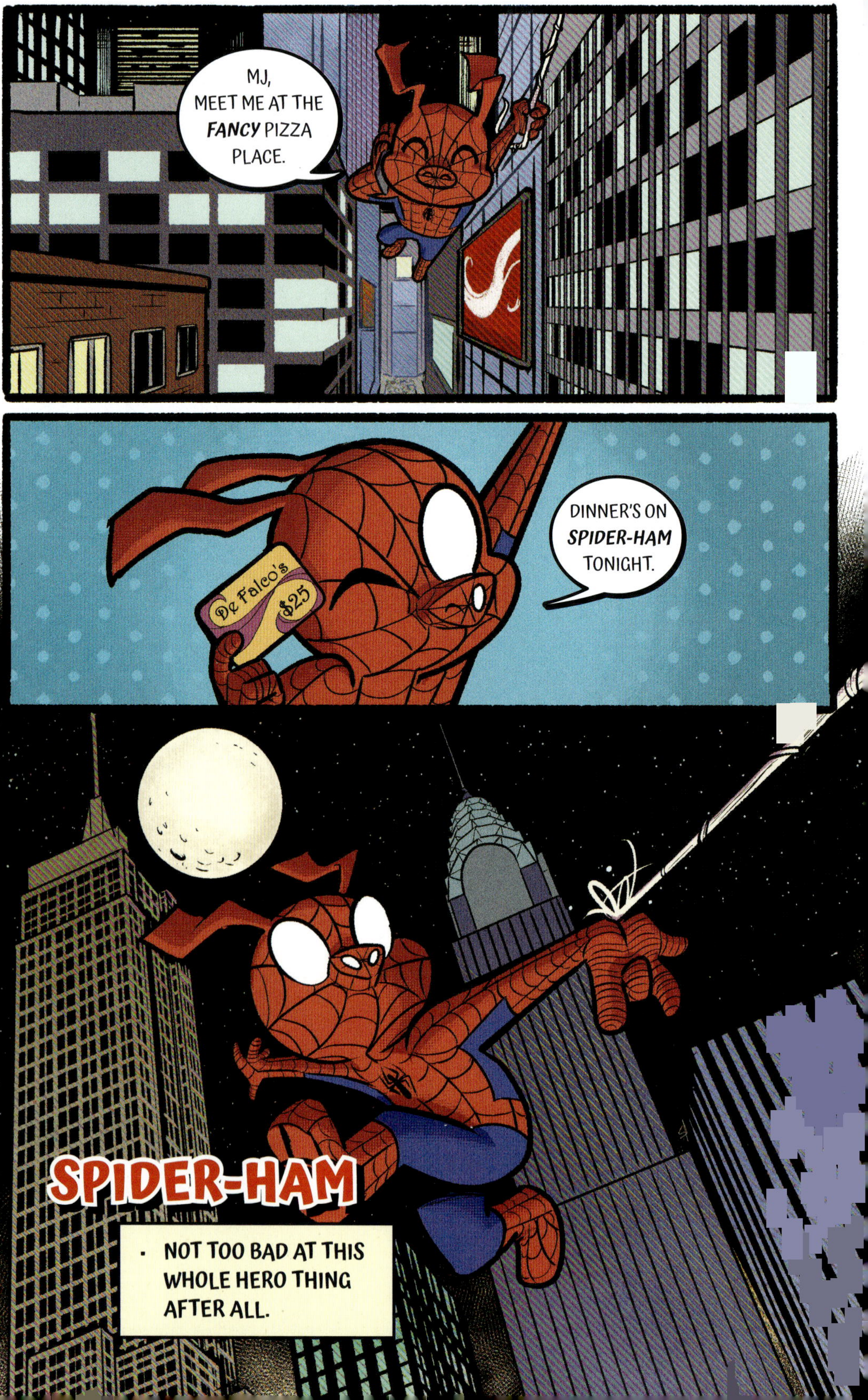
MJ, MEET ME AT THE FANCY PIZZA PLACE.
De Falco's $25
DINNER'S ON SPIDER-HAM TONIGHT.
SPIDER-HAM
• NOT TOO BAD AT THIS WHOLE HERO THING AFTER ALL.

THE
END

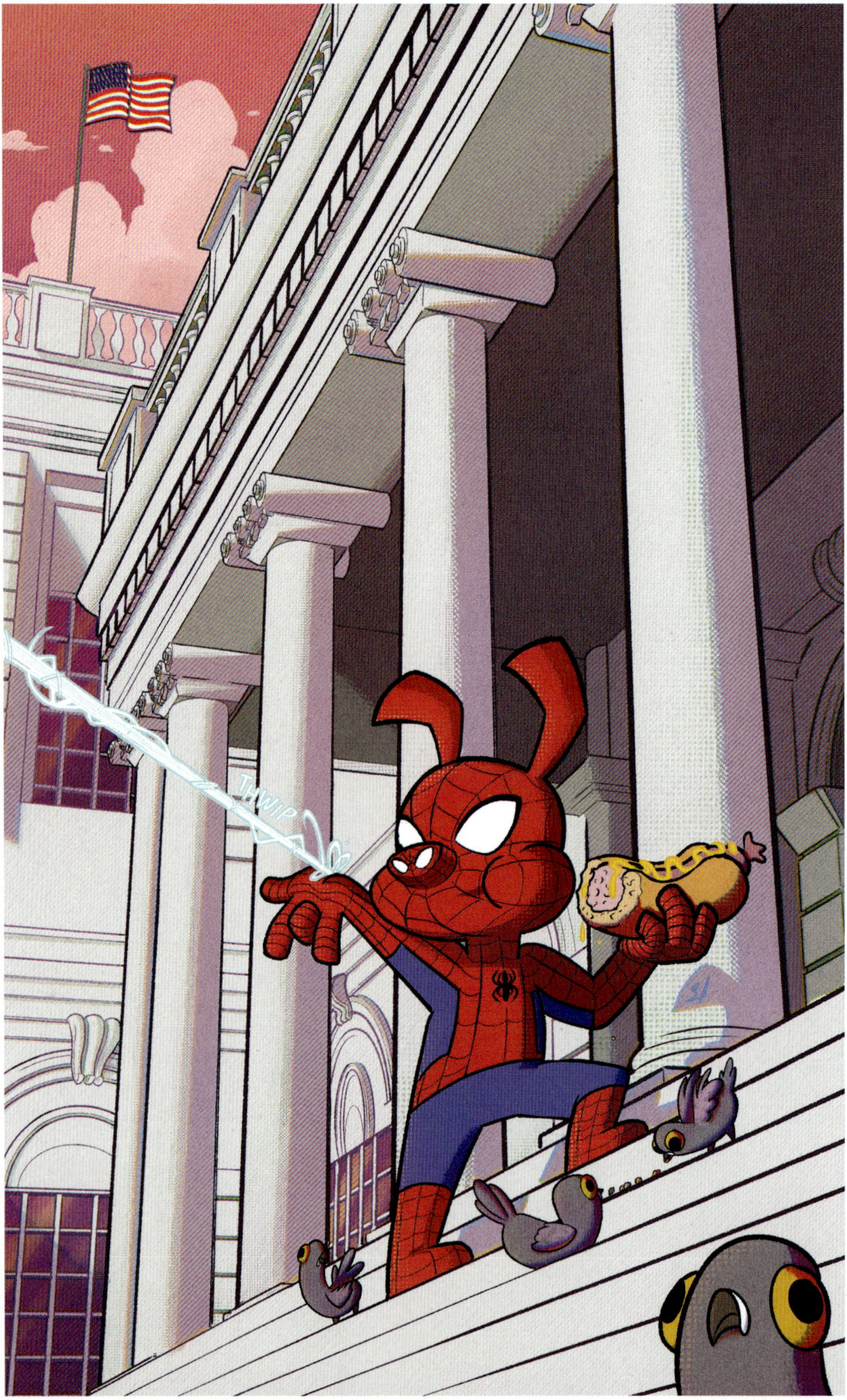
THWIP

SPOT THE DIFFERENCES: Can you spot the 6 differences?

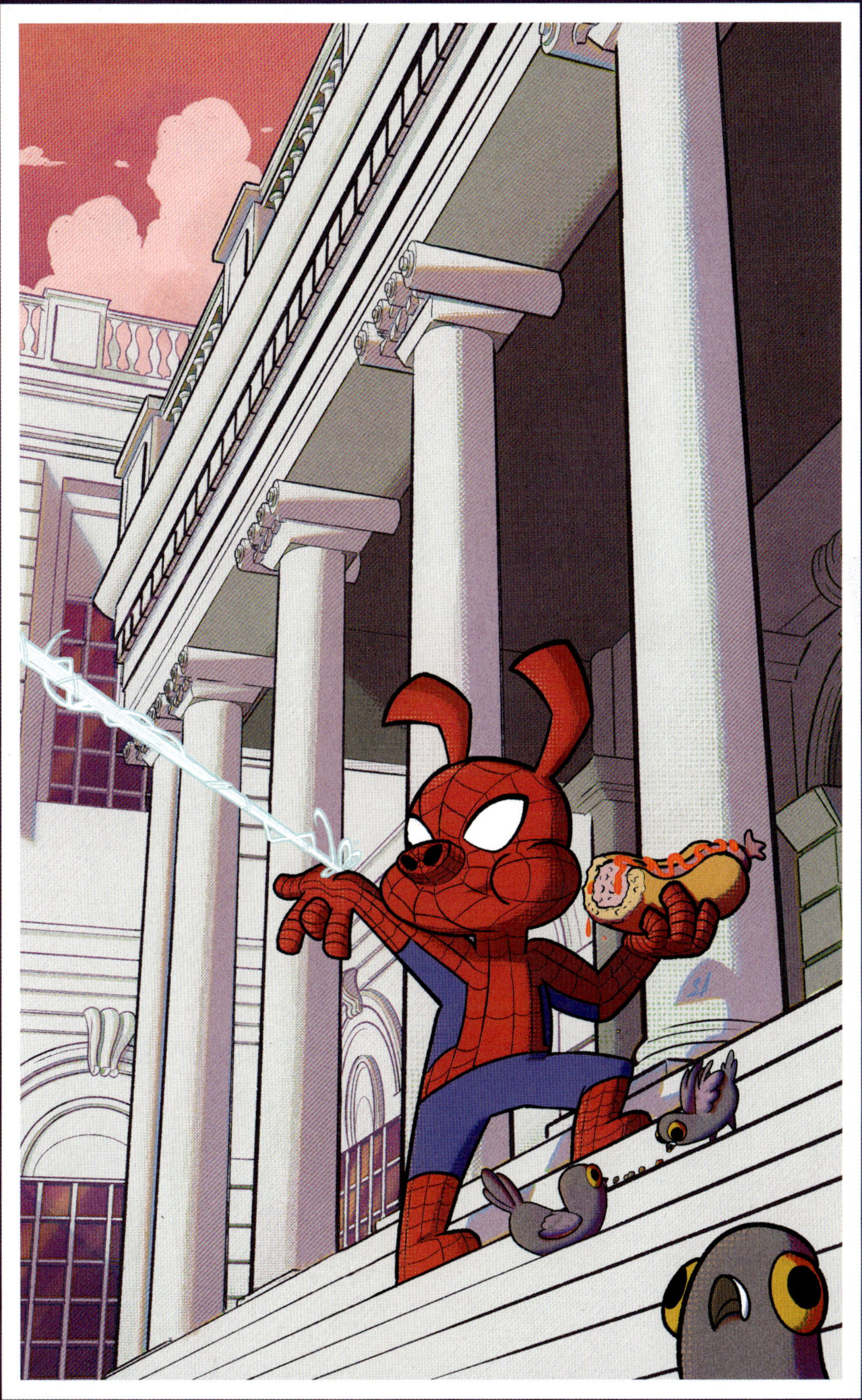

SPECIAL PREVIEW OF

Marvel Avengers Assembly #2: The Sinister Substitute!

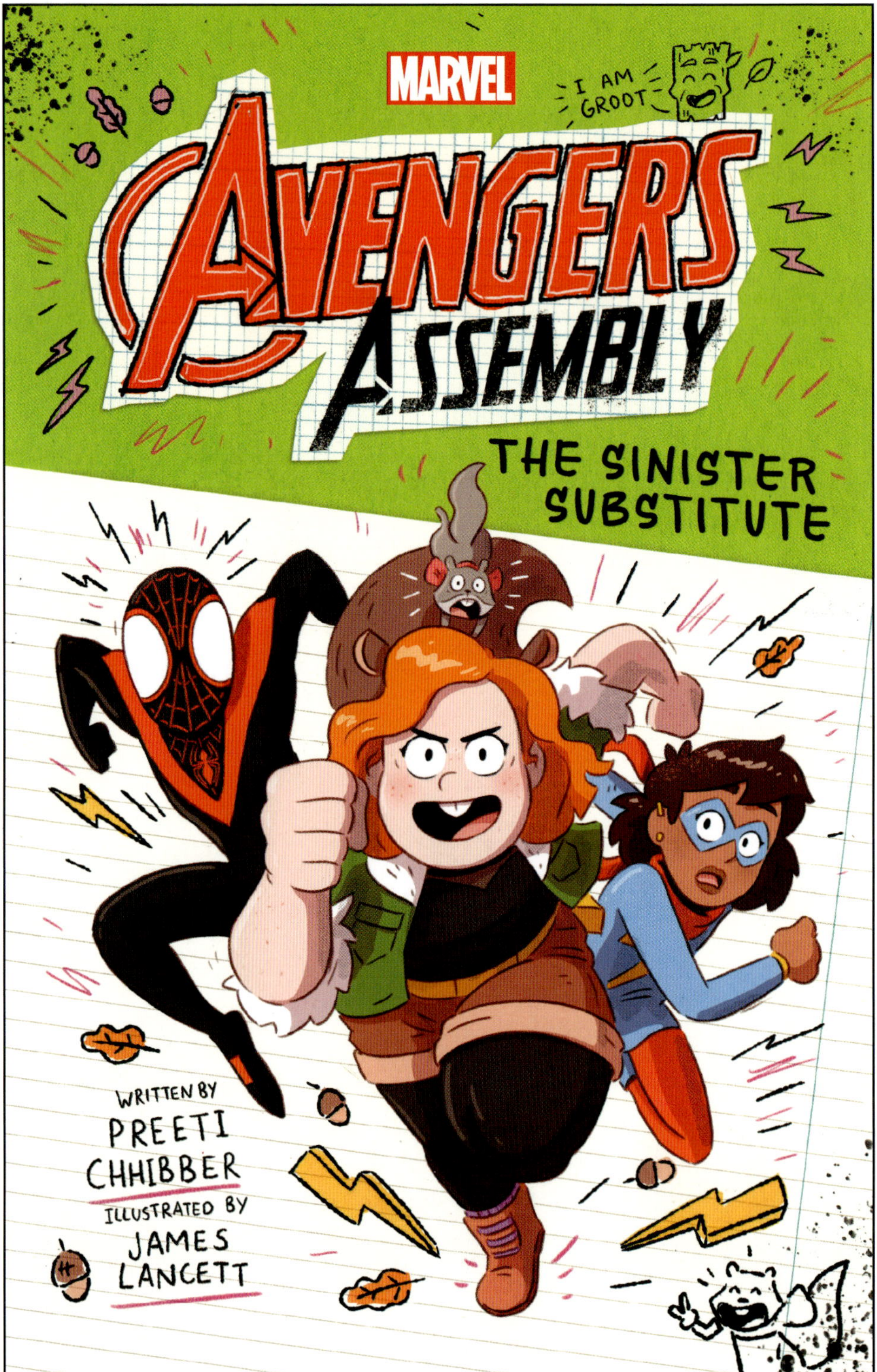
MARVEL
I AM GROOT
AVENGERS ASSEMBLY
THE SINISTER SUBSTITUTE
WRITTEN BY
PREETI CHHIBBER
ILLUSTRATED BY
JAMES LANCETT

CHAPTER 1

Yesterday! Was! Great!!!

Miles, Kamala, Evan, Tippy-Toe, and I are trying to get in as many Fun-Time Hang-Out sessions as we can before Avengers Institute starts again. I've already started today's scrapbook!

☑ Went to Luna Park on Coney Island and

☑ Ate too many hot dogs

MUNCH!
MUNCH!

☑ Followed by too much ice cream

LICK!

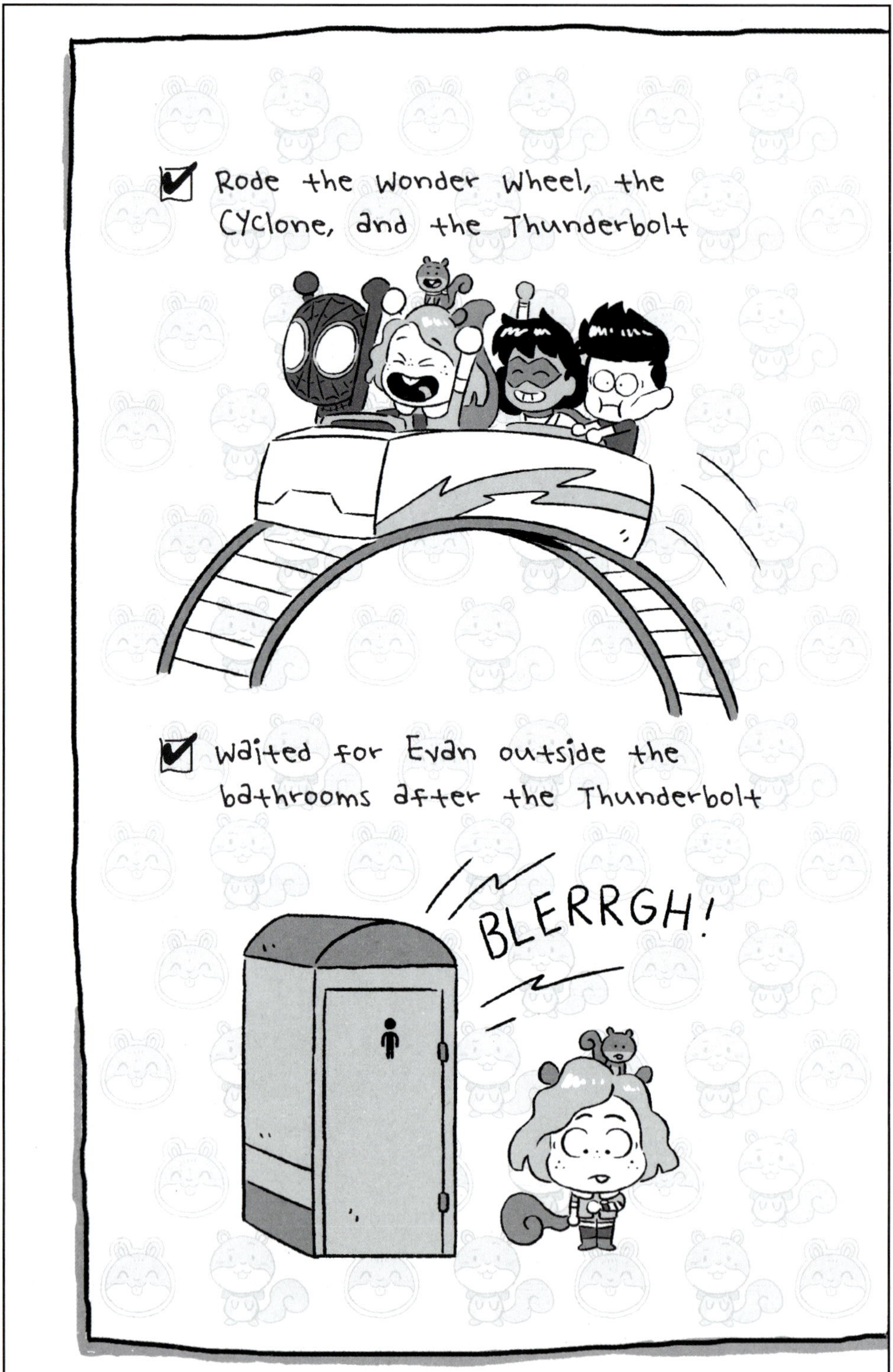
Rode the Wonder Wheel, the CYclone, and the Thunderbolt
Waited for Evan outside the bathrooms after the Thunderbolt
BLERRGH!

☑ Defeated a group of super villains who attacked the park

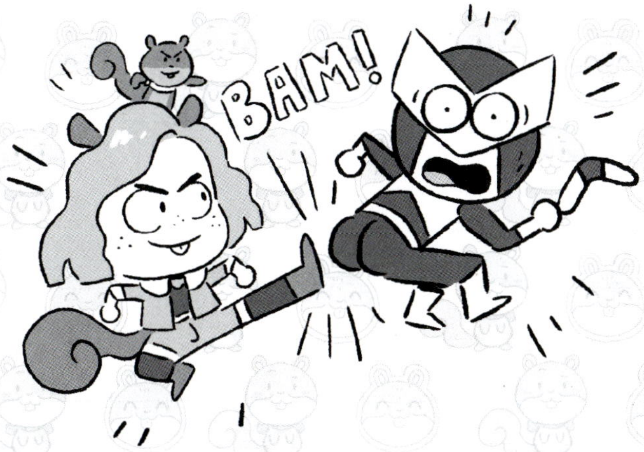
BAM!

☑ Watched the fireworks

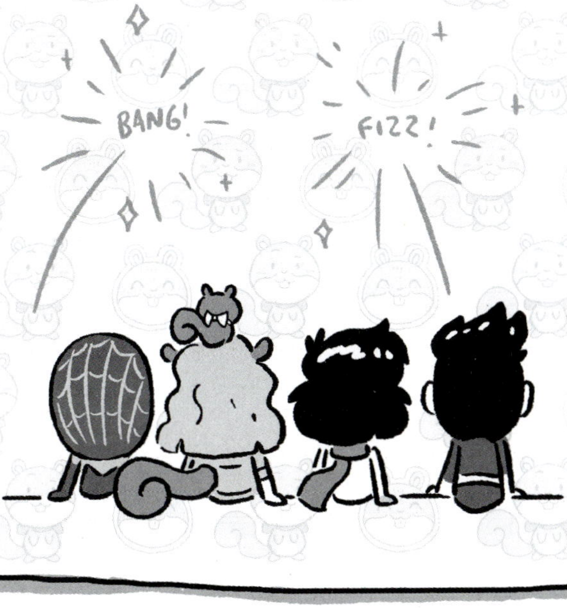
BANG!
FIZZ!

DOREEN'S NOTES

So, new year . . . Don't get me wrong, I think we're all excited to get back to class and learn some new stuff . . . or at least, me and Evan are definitely excited. Miles and Kamala are freaking out a bit because this semester is the science fair and they want to do a good job. But they're so good! I know they'll do an amazing job! I did the fair last semester and it was so easy—I created the code for a little robot squirrel and it was the cutest.

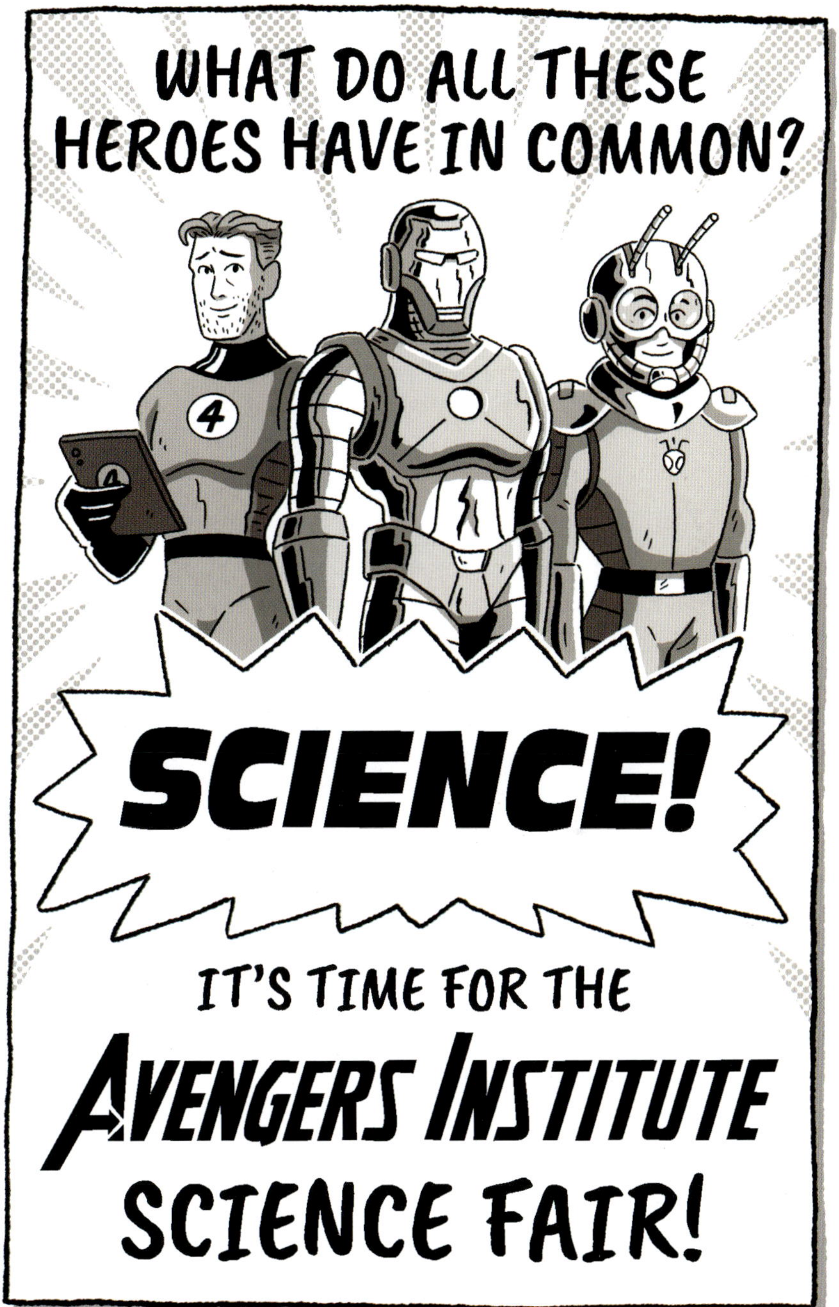
WHAT DO ALL THESE HEROES HAVE IN COMMON?
4
SCIENCE!
IT'S TIME FOR THE
AVENGERS INSTITUTE
SCIENCE FAIR!

DOREEN'S NOTES

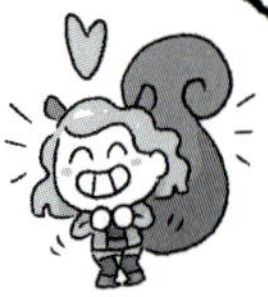

Anyway, we've been keeping the streets safe, no ifs, ands, or nuts about it. Sometimes that means team-building exercises! Today I got to pick the exercise and I called on a very special friend . . .

I feel like maybe I'm forgetting something? Like, there's something I'm supposed to be doing right this moment that I've totally forgot? Hmm . . .

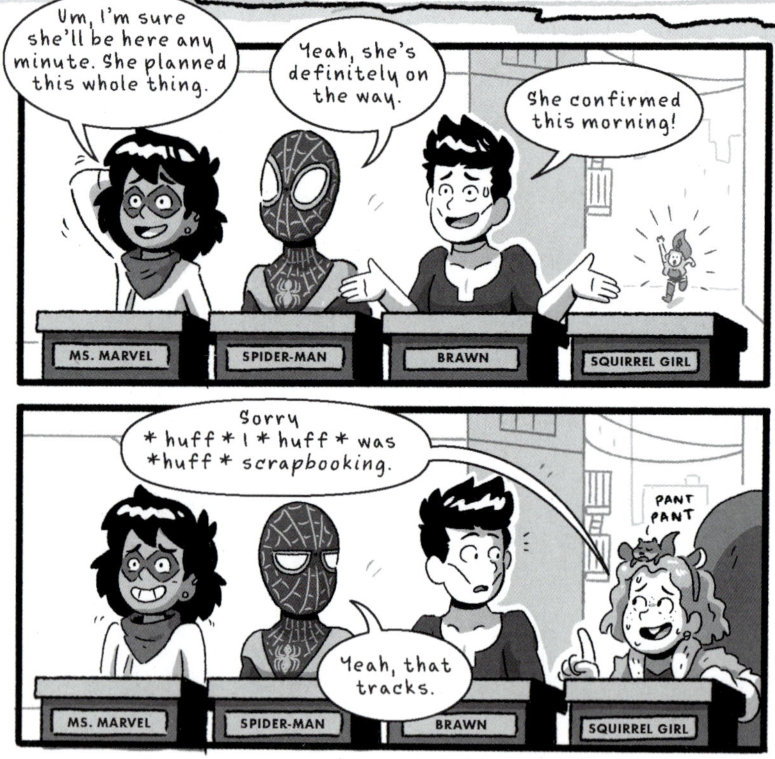

Um, I'm sure she'll be here any minute. She planned this whole thing.
Yeah, she's definitely on the way.
She confirmed this morning!
MS. MARVEL
SPIDER-MAN
BRAWN
SQUIRREL GIRL
Sorry *huff* I *huff* was *huff* scrapbooking.
PANT PANT
Yeah, that tracks.
MS. MARVEL
SPIDER-MAN
BRAWN
SQUIRREL GIRL

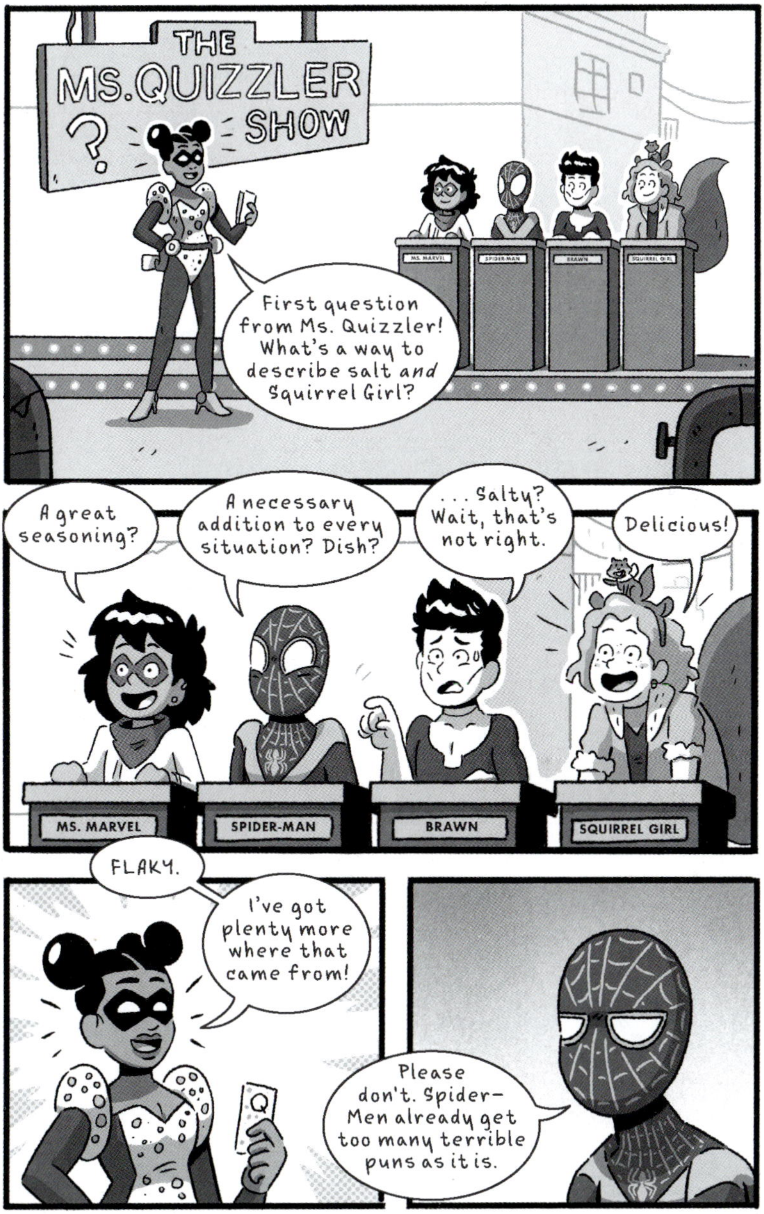
THE MS. QUIZZLER SHOW
MS. MARVEL
SPIDER-MAN
BRAWN
SQUIRREL GIRL
First question from Ms. Quizzler! What's a way to describe salt and Squirrel Girl?
A great seasoning?
A necessary addition to every situation? Dish?
. . . Salty? Wait, that's not right.
Delicious!
MS. MARVEL
SPIDER-MAN
BRAWN
SQUIRREL GIRL
FLAKY.
I've got plenty more where that came from!
Q
Please don't. Spider-Men already get too many terrible puns as it is.

MS. QUIZZLER'S NOTES FOR THE ULTIMATE QUIZZLER QUIZ SHOW

What do you call a lonely banana?

Ans: Akela

Note: Origin, Hindi. Akela means "alone," and the word <u>kela</u> means "banana."

What's a cat's favorite color?

Ans: Purrrple

Note: This isn't accurate, but Squirrel Girl taught me the joy of wordplay!

What is a thirsty man's favorite question?

Ans: Who?

Note: The chemical composition of water is H_2O: H-OO.

What do you call a cowardly octopus?

Ans: Spineless

Note: The octopus is one of nature's most well-known invertebrates.

From the desk of Dr. Bruce Banner

Avengers Assembly, it's time to SCIENCE!

Get ready to . . .

Have an awesome, science-filled time!
Use scientific equipment properly!
Learn how to invent
and experiment safely!
Know when to stop!

I know what you're thinking, but I only
have this to say:

Radiate? More like RADI-GREAT!

STEVE FOXE is the author of more than fifty comics and children's books for properties including Pokémon, Batman, Transformers, Adventure Time, Steven Universe, and Grumpy Cat. He lives in Queens with his partner and their dog, who is named after a cartoon character. He does not eat ham. Find out more at stevefoxe.com.

SHADIA AMIN is a Colombian comics artist currently living in the US. Her art aims to capture the fun of super heroes, fantasy, and life itself. Her works include BOOM!'s *The Amazing World of Gumball: The Storm*, Oni–Lion Forge's *Aggretsuko*, as well as collaborating on anthologies like *Alloy* from Ascend Comics and *Votes for Women* from Little Bird Press. Burgers are to her what hot dogs are to Spider-Ham.